SOMETHING *new*

ENTWINED IN YOU, BOOK ONE

ASHLEE ROSE

This book is dedicated to my wonderful husband Daniel, who, as always, told me to follow my dreams.

*Without you, this wouldn't have been possible and would have merely stayed a dream
Love you always x*

CHAPTER ONE

I was laying on the sofa slobbing with the cat.

I don't really like cats.

I'm more of a dog person. Tilly turned up four months ago when I moved into my flat and has never left. I sighed as I looked at her, padding her paws on my belly and purring. She wasn't that bad I suppose. My phone beeped, it was such an effort to move. I rolled my eyes, "Ugh, Tilly, move, I've got to get ready before bridezilla whips my arse."

My best friend of thirteen years is getting married in six weeks, 18th August to be exact. Laura had text me reminding me to be ready at eight p.m. sharp and not to be late. I am always late.

I slowly dragged myself away from the sofa, turned Friends off and made my way to the shower. I stepped out into the steamy box bathroom and wiped the mist away from the mirror. God, I looked awful, deep set bags lined my eyes and my dull hair laughed back at me. I am lucky I'm olive skinned, but lately I just feel pale. I hadn't been sleeping very well since I found my asshole ex, Jake, cheating.

We had been childhood sweethearts, and to be honest, I could see my future with him. Obviously, he couldn't.

I pulled a face as I caught my reflection in the mirror, *sort it out Freya*, my subconscious snarled at me. I shook away the thoughts. I threw my mid length hair into a towel and stood in front of the wardrobe. "What to wear, what to wear," I said to myself.

We were going to a little cocktail bar in London and then heading for dinner, nothing spectacular, but it was a night out. I opted for a black, thick strapped figure hugging midi dress. It wasn't too tight round my breasts and wasn't sticking to my thighs and bum. I have long legs and curvaceous bum and hips which complement my small waist. After missing my hair appointment, I decided to straighten my long auburn hair. I wasn't great when it came to make-up and hairstyles.

I then applied my foundation, bronzer, mascara and a re-application of my nude lipstick. I had one last look in the mirror before stepping into my heels.

I looked at the clock in the kitchen, seven-fifty. Wow, I was early. I smirked to myself, that's a first.

I poured myself a glass of white wine to enjoy while I was waiting. I looked at my phone and stared at the photo on my background. A photo of me and Jake in Venice was still on there, I just couldn't bring myself to change it. We looked so happy, we were so happy. Well I was. I still don't know what possessed him to do what he did and also how long it had been going on for. I didn't stay around long enough to find out.

I left Cambridgeshire where I grew up and moved to London, Highgate to be exact. It was the gorgeous terraced houses and the high-end independent boutiques that caught my eye.

Jake and I had lived in a little cottage in Elsworth. Everyone knows your business in Elsworth and I didn't want my failed relationship to be the talk of the village, and especially for my poor parents having to be constantly reminded of it. Moving to London was not ideal, rent's expensive but it's easy to get to work, plus my best friend Laura lives here.

After deciding to leave, I left my job in the quiet village law firm and was offered a new job in the city. The pay is good and pays the bills, so I can't really moan.

I ran my thumb over the screen, and before I could dwell on the past anymore, my buzzer rang. I had a quick look out the window and saw the taxi. I finished the rest of my wine, grabbed my clutch and my keys and ran out of the door.

I sat in the taxi, watching the city lights pass by. I had a little scroll through Instagram and noticed all the girls were already together. Balls. I looked at the time, eight-twenty. *It's fine,* I thought, *we will be there in ten minutes*; I hoped, anyway.

Twenty minutes later, after getting stuck in bloody traffic, I arrived at the cocktail bar. I was doing so well. I threw the taxi driver his money and wished him a good night. Stepping out of the taxi, the warm summer breeze hit me. I felt slightly tipsy, I'm a damn lightweight. I pulled my dress down, threw my hair over my shoulders and headed for the door. Laura was going to be so annoyed.

"Well, well, well, look who's finally arrived!" Laura teased.

"I'm sorry, so sorry! I got stuck in traffic, I was doing so well, I was dressed by seven-fifty!" I exclaimed.

"Oh shhh, it doesn't matter, you are here now. Here, drink this," she passed me a cosmopolitan, my favourite. Laura brushed through the group dancing to the music.

"Hey, you, love your dress," Brooke smiled.

Brooke was another friend who I grew up with. Laura, Brooke and I were the three musketeers throughout school. She had been married for two years now, and had a darling little princess called Lola. "This old thing?" I laughed. "Thank you, you look gorgeous my darling!"

She gave me a little twirl, "It's new. I haven't bought anything in over eighteen months because of my little Lola. Peter told me to go out today and have a pamper day, so I did just that. I went and got my hair styled, makeup done and treated myself to this outfit." She was wearing a very fitted black boob-tube jumpsuit. It hugged her curves perfectly, her long brown hair was curled and tumbled down past her chest.

I don't know how she was standing in her heels, they were ridiculously high. "Come on," she said, "let's go find the bride-to-be and get wasted!"

I rolled my eyes.

"What?!" she shrieked "I am making the most of this evening out, enjoy it whilst you can. Not that I would change it, I love being mummy to Lola, I really do." She looked down. "It's just nice to get out and just be me again, you do lose yourself being a mummy," she sighed.

"Hey, you haven't got to explain yourself to me. You enjoy your night off, you deserve it. Come on let's get wasted, as you put it," I replied, and she laughed.

I took her hand and followed the rest of the group, I only knew Laura's fiancé's sister, Zoe, and Laura's close work colleague Amy. The rest, I didn't have a clue who they were.

The night was in full swing, the cocktail making was so much fun. The nine of us were all on our way to being very drunk. We had a little VIP booth which kept us away from the crowds that started to form. I checked my phone, no messages, no missed calls. I pulled a face and threw my phone back into my clutch. Why would I have any messages? I gulped my drink down.

Laura came and slumped down next to me. "Hey Frey Frey, we've got to make our way to dinner and I'm really drunk and I don't think I'll be able to make it."

I smiled at her, "Come on you, let's get you up and get the gang together and we could try and make our way to dinner." Why Zoe would think about doing cocktails and then dinner was beyond me, most of the group were drunk and now we had to go and sit and try to act normally. Two taxis full of rowdy girls was just what these taxi drivers ordered. A ten-minute journey felt like forever with drunk Laura, who spent the time telling me she was going to be sick.

As we pulled up outside the restaurant, I decided to go in and cancel the reservation. The waiter was clearly annoyed, but he would have been more annoyed at having those wild animals sitting down in his restaurant. I called a cab and put Laura, Eloise, Trish and Charlotte safely in the back. They were far too drunk, and the only place for them was home.

Just as the cab was about to pull away, Zoe said she was going to jump in with them to make sure they weren't sick in his cab. Laura was hanging out the window trying to grab me "I don't want to go home," she wailed, "I'm not even that drunk, look at me. I am fine," she slurred.

I shook my head and laughed "I know you are sweetie, call me in the morning. Love you."

She sulked back into the cab and threw her hand up in the air at a poor attempt to wave, "Love you more!" she shouted as I watched the cab drive away.

The other two girls had disappeared, so it was only Brooke and I left. "We're not going home yet, are we? Let's go for a drink. There are loads of little bars and restaurants round here!"

I really just wanted to go home, but she was giving me puppy dog eyes. "Fine - let's go, one drink."

CHAPTER TWO

The next morning, I was awoken by the sun beaming through my windows. I rolled over to look at the time, 6:48am, ugh. I threw my head into my hands, it was banging. I don't remember much from last night.

As I slowly sat up, my head started to spin. I needed water. I slowly shuffled out of bed and threw my t-shirt on. After pouring myself a large glass of water and knocking back two anadin, I made my way back to my bedroom. I pulled the blinds that I had obviously forgotten to do last night and got back into bed.

Tilly was there all curled up and snoozing. I envied her.

I checked my phone again, a few drunken messages from Brooke that she had obviously sent when she got home. I was trying to think back about what I last remembered from last night, but my mind was too hazy. I wasn't used to caring for myself when I was hungover, usually Jake would be at my beck and call. He was good like that. I looked back at my phone and the picture, I really did miss him. I sighed and got back under the covers, but not before gulping the rest of my water. My mouth was so dry. I cuddled up with Tilly and slowly dozed back off.

I was awoken by my phone ringing, it was Laura. I looked at the time, it was 10:30. I sighed and slid the phone across. "Hey," I tried my best to sound awake and fresh, but I couldn't fool her.

"Oh, you sound rough! Where did you end up last night?!" she sounded great.

"Um, I don't really remember. My memory is in a bit of a haze at the moment, how are you feeling anyway?" I rolled over and got myself cosy again.

"Better than I deserve, I slept so well and I managed to convince the taxi driver to stop off at McDonalds on the way home, he said he didn't allow food in his cab so I told him that Trish would show him her boobs if he did."

I gasped. "No, you didn't?!"

She laughed, "Yup, and she did it as well, I knew she would. She's a nightmare once she's had a drink!" We couldn't stop laughing. "Anyway, I was calling to see if you wanted to meet for coffee, about midday?"

I looked back at the time; it gave me another hour in bed and just enough time for a shower and some dry shampoo. "Okay, I will meet you in Starbucks at 12, on the corner of Junction Street."

After saying our goodbyes, I called Brooke to see what

happened last night. Turns out we ended up in a local karaoke bar singing like drowned cats. After refusing to hand over the microphone back to another failed singer, we got kicked out. The humiliation hit me. Oh God, why do I feel the need to mix my drinks? Brooke sounded as rough as me; all I could hear in the background was Lola screeching "Mummy, mummy, mummy!" I told her I would let her go and call her in the week to arrange a meet up. I placed the phone face down on my bedside table and tried to get rid of the thumping headache by going back to sleep.

Fifteen minutes later, I was on Facebook stalking Jake's profile. It was a stab to the heart when I saw his profile picture of him and her. We only broke up four months ago and he is all loved up in a new relationship, and I am laying here with my cat, feeling and looking like death, stalking him. I started thinking back to when I found out about him cheating.

I was away for a couple of nights for a family party, my dad's side live in Devon, and Jake said he couldn't come with me as his boss wouldn't agree his leave, I scoffed thinking back at it. We were meant to stay for two nights and travel back on the Sunday evening, but my mum was unwell with flu, so we decided to travel home Saturday morning instead. It was late afternoon when we arrived home, and mum and dad dropped me to the cottage. I was happy to see Jake's car on the drive, I had only been gone a night and I missed him. I grabbed my suitcase out the back of dad's car, threw my tatty bag over my shoulder and waved goodbye. As I pulled my little suitcase up our driveway, I couldn't wait to see him.

As I opened our door, what I could have waited to see was my boyfriend's sweaty, naked body over some girl, on my new rug in front of our fire. I dropped my bag to the floor, he looked over his shoulder. Sheer panic and regret in his eyes. She looked up at me from underneath him, she had short pixie hair, and cute features, but she was nothing special. "Freya..." he mumbled, I just stared at him.

I reached for my glass key bowl that was to the side of the door on a table and threw it at the floor. I was heartbroken and angry, but I wasn't going to cry in front of him, and especially not her. It took everything in me not to cave.

After what felt like a lifetime, I cleared my throat "Okay, so I'm going now. Once you're finished with her, get the rug cleaned, actually just throw it out and don't bother calling me." I picked up my bag up off the floor, grabbed my suitcase and turned for the door.

"Freya, please, it's not what it looks like!"

I turned back round, "Sorry? What does it look like then Jake? Because to me, it looks like my boyfriend is shagging some tart on my new rug, in our house and I have just walked in and caught you. Is that not what is happening here?!"

I didn't realise, but my voice had been getting higher and higher. He couldn't even say anything, he was scrambling around trying to get his clothes together, she was trying to pull my throw off of my sofa to cover herself. I shook my head "You deserve each other."

I turned for the door, slamming it behind me. I reached around my bag for my phone. "Mum, can you come and get me?" I tried to sound fine, but I could tell by her voice she knew something was wrong.

I didn't want to stand by the cottage so I started walking down the road they would drive into, after about ten minutes I could see dad's jeep. The tears started to fill my eyes.

As dad pulled over my mum jumped out the car "Darling, what is it? What's happened?" she ushered me into the car and sat in the back with me. I couldn't hold it anymore; the tears were flowing down my cheeks. "Harry, pull over. You can't drive while she is like this." She pulled me into her, she stroked my hair "It's okay Freya, come on, tell mum what's happened."

I wiped my eyes and sat up. I took a deep breath "It's Jake, I have just caught him having sex with some girl in the living room, on my new rug."

Mum just gasped and put her hands over her mouth.

Dad was seething, "That clown, who does he think he is doing this to our daughter? I'm going back there, he is not getting away with this!"

I looked at mum.

"Now Harry, calm down. Going back there isn't going to solve anything at the moment, our main priority is Freya, we need to get her home and away from this situation."

Dad looked shocked at what mum had said, "Rose, he has betrayed my little girl, how can I just drive away?" Mum just gave him her look and he hung his head in defeat. "Fine," he grumbled, "but he won't get away with this." I smiled at mum as we headed down the lanes.

I just wanted to get home. I know my cottage was home, but I wanted to go to my childhood home. Just home.

I threw my phone down and dragged my bum out of bed. Tilly was still sleeping, oh to be a cat. I walked into my bathroom and turned the shower on – I let the water wash away my thoughts. Why do showers feel so good? I stepped out, brushed my teeth, pulled my hair into a messy bun and walked into my tip of a bedroom. I really need to tidy up, but first coffee.

I pulled on my good old river island jeans and a plain grey t-shirt and slipped into my flip-flops. I said bye to the cat, she didn't respond, just moved slightly. I grabbed my tatty bag, threw my purse and phone in and walked out of the door to meet Laura.

I left the flat and walked along the street. My little flat was near the station which was ideal for my job. It was noisy but comforting. After the sale went through on the cottage, I put the money into saving and opted for renting.

As you walk in the door of my flat, there's a little hallway, at the end of the hallway and to the right is a small kitchen area with a breakfast bar which separates the living room from the kitchen. My bedroom is off the living room to the left, and the bathroom is next to my bedroom, opposite the kitchen. It's not great, but I love it.

I crossed the road and made my way into Starbucks. There Laura was, sitting fresh eyed, looking as beautiful as ever, sipping her coffee. I sat down in front of her and placed my hands around my coffee. I needed this.

"So, how are you?" she said with a smile.

"I've been better," I admitted. I didn't want to bring the Jake story up again, that's all my life is about. I'm 28, single with a cat and barely got my life together. "What are you and Tyler doing today?"

Tyler was Laura's doting fiancé. He was a hopeless romantic whose world revolved around her. They met back in university, Tyler was a stock broker, Laura was in media. "Not a lot really," she sipped her white skinny decaf coffee, "we've got to go and tie some loose ends up with the groom's party's suits, nothing exciting. What about you?"

I tried to think up something but nothing popped into my hungover head, "Will probably crawl back to bed and watch a Sex and The City, and maybe do some work that I should have done Friday." She rolled her eyes at me. Laura got me a job at the magazine company she worked for, You

Magazine. When everything happened with Jake, I was an assistant to Jools Hearn. It wasn't my dream job, but it was work. My dream is to write, whether that be blogging, columns for magazines, or even a book.

My foot is in the door here which is great, but my boss is hard on me. I quickly changed the subject, "Not long till the wedding! When are our final fittings for the bridesmaid dresses?"

She was tapping away on her phone tutting to herself "Next Saturday, I managed to get us in a week earlier, is that good for you?"

I told her of course it was fine. I can't believe she and Tyler are getting married in six weeks. They have chosen a beautiful venue back up near Elsworth. Laura wanted to be back near home with her family.

"Have you found a plus one yet?" she chirped. I gave her the look, the look that she knew very well. "It's okay, we have six weeks to find you a date. I can't cancel the numbers now; I sort of kept your plus one in case you got back with Jake."

I nearly choked on my coffee, "Sorry, what?"

She looked into her cup, "Well, I did. I thought you would take him back, I mean his is the only guy you have ever loved, the only guy you have ever – you know... had sex with..."

I scowled, "So what?"

She gave me an apologetic look. "Freya, I didn't mean it like that!"

19

I finished my coffee and slammed the mug down on the table. "I'm going, I've got work to do before the dragon fires my arse, then I will be jobless as well as boyfriend-less." She went to stand up and stop me, but she knows me too well. She sat back down in her seat and threw her head back. I didn't even look at her. I picked my tatty bag up, threw it over my shoulder and stormed out of Starbucks. I am such a diva at times.

CHAPTER THREE

After sitting sulking for a couple of hours whilst stuffing my face with Ben & Jerry's ice-cream and bingeing on Sex & The City, I decided it was time to go over my notes from my meeting with Jools.

I walked into my dive of a bedroom - *it really does need to be cleaned.* I quickly got rid of that thought, grabbed my Mac out of the bedside cabinet and slumped myself back down on the sofa. I opened my email and started writing my notes to Jools.

After what seemed like forever, I proof read and sent. I decided to have a scroll through the magazines website, before I knew it I was on the vacancy page.

There, in all its glory was a position for a website blogger. I jumped at my chance and opened another email. Jools was editor of You Media and if I could get her attention with a good article, I might be in with a chance at this job. It was a shot in the dark, but I decided to give it ago.

To: Jools (Jools.Hearn@you.co.uk)

CC:

From: Freya (Freya.Greene@you.co.uk)

Subject: Vacancy   for   Website   Blogger   at YouMagazine.co.uk

18TH June 2018 at 14:03

Dear Jools,

Please can I have some more information on what would be required to apply for this job? I am very interested in pursuing my dream in writing and would love this opportunity to be reviewed for this vacancy.

I look forward to hearing from you,

Kind Regards

Freya Greene

Assistant to Jools Hearn

You Magazine

Oxford Street

London

W1D 1BS

www.youmagazine.co.uk

Sent.

My heart was in my mouth, I doubt she would even consider me but if I didn't do it now, then I don't know when my next opportunity would be. I ventured back into my bedroom "Right, let's get this over with," I muttered to Tilly.

An hour later, and I had a room again. I was feeling rather chuffed with myself, my bedside cabinets were polished, my carpet was hoovered, my dirty washing picked up and moved to the laundry basket, bed made and clothes away. It was three pm. I decided to go out and have a little look around the shops before they closed.

I ended up in a furniture shop just round the corner to my flat. I was aimlessly walking around and dreaming about re-decorating my flat when before I knew it, I bumped into someone, face on.

"Oh my god, I am so sorry!" I felt myself go red. I looked up, my jaw hit the floor.

"Hey, it's okay, don't worry, I wasn't looking where I was going either!" We both laughed. "I'm Ethan, so, what you in here for? Looking for bits for you and your husband's house?"

I scoffed, "Husband!? – No, no husband. Not even a boyfriend, just a cat. Tilly the cat," oh dear, Freya, seriously – mouth – stop.

"Oh," he seemed taken back by my outburst. He probably thinks I'm a right loser, he's in here with his girlfriend who's probably looking at matching his and hers towels no doubt and here I am goofing about my cat.

Then after what seemed like a lifetime of silence he said "I love cats - I do like dogs, but I love cats. So, no boyfriend or husband, it must be my lucky day. I have just moved here, bought a nice little flat around the corner, hence why I am in here, at three thirty on a Sunday afternoon, looking at plates."

I smiled at him.

"What's your name then?"

"Freya."

He smiled back at me. "Nice to meet you, officially, Freya. So, can I get your number? Maybe we can go for a drink sometime, if that's okay with you?" I was too busy staring at his beautiful hazel eyes, his hair was blonde and curly, his glorious tanned skin, his stubble across his chin and from what I could see under his polo, a very nice body. "Err, Freya? Did I cross the line?"

"Um, nope. Sorry. Yes, of course." We exchanged numbers and then we carried on in conversation for a good fifteen minutes.

"I better go, don't want to miss out on these plates!"

We said our goodbyes, and I left the store.

I walked with a skip in my step as I went back to the flat, I kept checking my phone. I wasn't going to text him first, he said he would like to go for a drink with me, so, he can be the one to text. I nodded and smiled to myself.

It had just gone seven. I decided to jump in the shower

and wash my hair for the morning. I sorted my clothes and laid them on my chair in the corner of the room. Again, I checked my phone. Nothing from Ethan.

I opened my Mac, just to see if I had received an email from Jools. I wasn't getting my hopes up, but it couldn't hurt, could it? As I scrolled through the junk mail – Domino's pizza, Just Eat, Hungry House... I realised I needed to go on a diet. Just as I was about to give up, there it was, a little unread email from Jools Hearn. I couldn't help it, I wiggled in my seat with excitement.

To: Freya (Freya.Greene@you.co.uk)
CC: Laura HR (Laura.Henshaw@you.co.uk)
*From: Jools (**Jools.Hearn@you.co.uk**)*
Subject: RE: Vacancy for Website Blogger at YouMagazine.co.uk
18TH June 2018 at 15:43

Dear Freya,

This is a web-based position. We need somebody who can give us a new article every week on fashion, food, love and adventure. I would be happy to forward your details to HR, but please, don't get your hopes up.

You Media are looking for a particular style of writing. Please can you write a 300-word piece on yourself and send it to me.

Laura,

Please arrange an interview for Freya Greene at your earliest convenience.

Regards,
Jools Hearn
Editor
You Magazine
Oxford Street
London
W1D 1BS
www.youmagazine.co.uk

Okay, it could have been worse.

I have been given a chance, a chance to hopefully move up in my career. I picked Tilly up and had a dance with her around my bedroom. She screeched and then hissed at me. Fine, I thought. I threw her back on the bed. Miserable.

I walked to the kitchen and poured myself my last glass of wine, I am starting my health kick from tomorrow. I heard my phone beep but ignored it as it would only be Laura quizzing me about Jools's email. I sat on the side, enjoying my glass of wine while pondering about my future, imagine.

Me. Writing for You Magazine.

I was in dreamland when I heard my phone beep again. I just wanted to enjoy my glass of wine while day dreaming, in peace.

I slid off the worktop and picked my phone up off my desk. One message from Laura – ignored. One message from an unknown number. I entered my pass code and opened the message:

Hey You,

Sorry for not contacting you sooner, been caught up with work calls.

So that drink? How about tomorrow, after work? I work in the city, so maybe we could meet somewhere in-between? Let me know, Ethan X

I jumped up and down on the spot, completely forgetting about my wine that was now all over me. I was just about to punch a reply, but I stopped myself. At least give it an hour Freya.

Tilly and I lay cuddled up on the sofa watching the usual boring stuff on TV. I leant over to get my phone and I quickly typed out a reply:

Hey!

Yes, tomorrow is good for me. How about we meet in Liverpool Street, grab a drink before our train?

6pm work for you? Let me know, Freya X

I had a quick look at Laura's message, she basically apologised for being a douche. I just replied with a simple "X" – I couldn't be bothered with this tonight. Ethan replied almost instantly agreeing to the time.

It was nine pm. I decided to write my 300-word submission and get it sent, half hour later I was still staring at a blank email – *you can do this Freya, clear your mind and write.*

To: Jools (Jools.Hearn@you.co.uk)

CC:

*From: Freya (**Freya.Greene@you.co.uk**)*

Subject: 300 Word Submission

18th June 2018 at 22:12

Dear Jools,

Please see below submission:

Hi, I'm Freya. Let me give you a little run down on where I am at this moment in my life. I am 28 years old, I live in Highgate, London. I used to live in Elsworth, Cambridgeshire until I caught my douche bag of a boyfriend of 12 years sleeping with a mystery blonde, who I later found out was a receptionist at his garage where he worked as a mechanic.

So, I got up and left, I came to London where I was given an opportunity to work at a magazine company where I am hoping to pursue my dream career of writing.

My ex-boyfriend did try and get in contact with me a few times, but after changing my number and taking myself away from this little village where everyone knew my business and what had happened, I decided to cut him off. Last I heard, (because I Facebook stalked him) he is still happily shacked up with the blonde who ruined our forever.

Anyway, I promise to keep you informed of all my adventures, fashion tips (not that I have many at the moment so bear with me) and also, my new love life.

I have recently been asked out by somebody I bumped into at a furniture shop. We are going out for a little drink after work tomorrow. If this works out for me, then you will get to read and laugh, maybe cry sometimes with me.

I've got my best friend's wedding coming up where I am Maid of Honour! I'm also an avid wine drinker.

I love dogs but ended up with a stray cat four months ago that has never left. Hopefully you can help me with things, as much as I will try and help you, try. I really will. We will become a team.

Kind Regards

Freya Greene

Assistant to Jools Hearn
You Magazine
Oxford Street
London
W1D 1BS
www.youmagazine.co.uk

I had a quick read through what I had written and sent it without hesitation. What will be, will be.

I went through the flat, turned everything off, fed the cat, locked the front door and got myself into bed.

As I was dozing off, my mind drifted to Ethan. His warm eyes, I could get lost in them, his sun kissed olive skin, his strong, but soft jawline with perfectly trimmed stubble – I just couldn't get over how good looking he was, my mind drifted to various scenarios.

Before I knew it, I was dreaming of having sex with him.

I woke myself up, sweating. It had been about nine months since Jake and I last had sex, I have never been with anyone else. These feelings that were running through my body were new to me. Jake and I were so used to each other that it just became the norm.

The same positions, the same night, the same time.

I always thought it was good, but I had nothing to compare it to. I ran to the bathroom and splashed my face with cold water. I dried my face and headed back to bed. Hopefully no more dreaming about Ethan.

I did go to bed with a smile on my face, can't even lie about it.

CHAPTER FOUR

I got ready for work in the morning. I felt so anxious about seeing Jools after I submitted my email to her. I checked myself in the mirror, pencil skirt, white sleeveless shirt and a pair of heels. I checked my phone, 7:30am, time to go.

While I was sitting on the train, I started thinking about meeting Ethan tonight. For the first time in a long while, I had butterflies. Who knows, this could be it?

I arrived at Oxford Street at 08:50am, run to Starbucks and grabbed mine and Jools's coffees. Skinny vanilla latte for me (I do try) and a black tall Americano for her. I walked into the office at bang on 9 o'clock.

I dumped my bag on the floor, placed my coffee by my phone and walked into Jools's office. "Morning Jools," I said with a smile on my face, "how are you this morning?"

She looked up from her computer "Well, isn't somebody in a good mood?!" I gave her an awkward smile. "So, I read your email, it was okay, not great, but okay." I sighed. "But – I am going to give you a chance, to be honest, I only had like, five emails and they were worse than yours. You have three months to impress me. I am still going to run the vacancy on the website, if somebody comes along and blows me away, then they will take this position. I still require you to be my assistant, this job needs to be done in your own time. So, is there anything new in your boring life since your boyfriend cheated on you?"

I was used to her being a bit of a bitch, but this, wow. This was a whole new level of bitch. I fidgeted on the spot, "Err, well I met someone in a shop near me, we are going for a drink tonight..."

"Excellent," she smiled, "I want to know all about it, I want your email sent to me by 11pm tonight, I would like you to send me an email all week at the same time so we are a week ahead of ourselves." She looked back at her computer. "I also want all the juicy gossip, none of this sugar coating crap. I want it all."

I agreed and told her she wouldn't be disappointed. Then I thanked her for giving me this opportunity. I couldn't believe it, it had actually happened.

"That will be all, now go."

I scuttled out of her room and sat at my desk. I opened my emails and scrolled through the new pieces for the magazine. Every week we have a new topic, on a Monday I have to scroll through, find the best fit for our topic and then give them to Jools. Once she has decided, I email the writer, change a few bits and send a copy to the editing team. I was so excited, I couldn't concentrate, I had to tell someone, so I emailed Laura:

> *To: Laura HR (Laura.Henshaw@you.co.uk)*
> *From: Freya (Freya.Greene@you.co.uk*
> *Subject: GOSSIP*
> *19TH June 2018 at 09:35*
>
> *Laura,*
>
> *I have some juicy gossip to tell you!!!!!!*
>
> *Freya Greene*
> *Assistant to Jools Hearn*
> *You Magazine*
> *Oxford Street*
> *London*
> *W1D 1BS*
> *www.youmagazine.co.uk*

I started going back through my emails, all of a sudden Jools bellowed my name from her office making me jump. "FREYA! Get in here!"

I pushed off my desk and ran into her office. "Everything okay!?" I was panicked, God this woman intimidates me.

"Fine, I want another coffee, not that crap you bought me, go make me one please." I get her a Starbucks every morning, so why now? I went to walk away. "Wait, I'm not finished."

I turned back on my heel and faced her.

"Our CEO over at Coles Enterprise has called me to let me know that CPH's assistant has gone on long term sick, they need cover for a week. So, I mentioned you and told them that you are not overly busy, so you would take over. She used to do five book manuscripts a day, so I expect that or more from you, understood?"

Was she actually joking with me? I was so angry, I am run off my feet with her, and now she wants me to take on another full-time role, "Sorry, what's CPH?" I asked.

She looked over her computer screen and said, "City Publishing House, Mr Cole took over that company a year ago, they are our sister company."

I nodded. "Okay then."

"Her emails have been re-directed to you, so please start going through them. Mr. Cole will be over this afternoon for a brief meeting with you, he likes to interview his staff. I'm not sure how he has the time, if I'm honest," she mumbled to herself.

I nodded and walked back to my desk. How the bloody hell am I going to do this? *Who's Mr Cole?* I wondered, so I decided to give him a quick look up on the internet.

As I was typing his name, I was expecting a fifty-ish year old man to pop up. What I wasn't expecting was a handsome, seductive, green eyed god starting back at me. I was grateful for an early night last night and the fact I had actually decided to do my hair.

I thanked whoever was watching over me in my head.

He wasn't the Editor, of course he wasn't, he was the owner of Cole Enterprise, as well as You Magazine and CPH. Mr Carter Lewis Cole, 32 years old, took over his father's company when he passed away in 2009. His father had named his company after their family name. Cole Enterprises finds struggling businesses and buys them out of their financial difficulty. There was a small list of other companies he owned. All I was interested in was the magazine and the publishing house.

I was literally drooling at my desk when Jools snapped, "Freya, COFFEE!"

Oh, bloody hell, I forgot. I ran to the staff kitchen and made her a black coffee and put it on her desk "Sorry!" I said with a little smile.

I got back to my desk and noticed an email from Laura.

To: Freya (Freya.Greene@you.co.uk
CC:
From: Laura HR (Laura.Hearne@you.co.uk)
Subject: RE: GOSSIP
19th June 2018 at 10:27

Oh! You want to talk to me now stroppy knickers!??!?!

Laura Hearne
HR Manager
You Magazine
Oxford Street
London
W1D 1BS
www.youmagazine.co.uk

I rolled my eyes, to be honest, I did send her a blunt email message back. I typed a quick response.

To: Laura HR (Laura.Henshaw@you.co.uk)
CC:
From: Freya (Freya.Greene@you.co.uk)
Subject: RE: RE: GOSSIP
19th June 2018 at 10:30

Oh, quit being a whinge bag will you! I have even more gossip now. Can you do lunch? 12:30 – can only have half an hour, you will understand why when I see you. Meet at the little deli on the corner?? xx

Freya Greene
Assistant to Jools Hearn

You Magazine
Oxford Street
London
W1D 1BS
www.youmagazine.co.uk

Couple of kisses on the end should soften the blow. Drama queen. She replied back almost instantly, agreeing to meet me at 12:30 at our local deli.

I started reading through the emails from CPH, making notes of the ones I thought would catch his eye.

Before I knew it, it was 12:30. I locked my PC, grabbed my bag and ran out of my office. The deli was a five-minute walk from our office; the staff knew Laura and I. We had been going there since I started at the job back in April.

I was greeted by Antonio who took me to where Laura was sitting at our usual table under the big window looking out at busy Oxford Street. I gave her a smile as I sat down "Are you okay?" I asked.

"I'm stressed out with the wedding, but that is going to take more than a half hour lunch!" Antonio came back over with two ice cold white wine spritzers, perfect. He's so good looking, tanned, dark skinned and dark eyes. His smile is slightly crooked but he really is handsome, his wife is a lucky woman.

I ordered a mozzarella and sun-dried tomato panini; Laura ordered a Greek salad. "Come on then, what's the gossip?" she asked me.

As I took a bite into my panini, I said "Well, I've got a date tonight..." before I could finish my sentence she was squealing. I didn't realise I had bought a pig to lunch with me.

I shook my head while taking another bite of my panini. "Anyway, I'm meeting him in Liverpool Street at 6pm for a drink..."

"What's he like, what's he like?" she mumbled, shovelling a massive mouthful of salad in her mouth. We really didn't have any manners.

"Tall, blonde, handsome..." I laughed, "he is extremely easy on the eye. Anyway, my other bit of gossip is the dragon pulled me in the office today, I have been offered the writing job on the website on a temporary basis for three months until she basically finds someone better suited for the role."

"That bitch," she shook her head "who does she think she is?"

"My boss, Laura," I rolled my eyes, "anyway, then she called me back into the office about half hour later, telling me that our sister company City Publishing House's assistant had gone on long term sick. I had to take over her role which entails reading and submitting five manuscripts and sending off to their editor, and I've got a meeting at 2pm with the editor, so I thought, oh no, it's only the owner of the company – I looked him up and Laura, he is so good looking – and single may I add..."

Laura's mouth dropped open. "She wants you to do WHAT? You are only one person; how does she expect you to carry out two people's fulltime jobs? Surely, she's paying you, more right? And oh my god, I need to see this man, try and take a sneaky photo for me!"

I just shrugged, I hadn't actually asked her, and I don't think I wanted to.

I suddenly wasn't hungry, I was now anxious and my stomach was in knots.

"No, I am not taking a photo, just google him, like any normal person. I've got to go sweet, back to the dragon's den!" I waved Antonio over and paid the bill, my treat for being a dick to Laura. Plus, it wouldn't break the bank. I wasn't swimming in money, but this job did pay well, yes, rent was expensive but I don't really have a social life, so it gradually builds up. I do have my savings from my sale of the cottage, but I'm leaving that until I find a property I really want, or, when I find the man I want to share a home with.

I gave Laura a kiss on the cheek, waved bye to Antonio and walked back to the office. I was so nervous again.

CHAPTER FIVE

Before going back to my desk, I ran to the toilet. I brushed my hair and tousled my loose curls, re-applied some nude lipstick and added a little more bronzer, just to get my glow back and sprayed some of my favourite perfume (Chanel No.5, can't beat a classic.)

I walked back out to the office and opened up my emails, I saw one from Jools simply saying she was out for the afternoon and to have the five manuscripts ready and on her desk. She also went on to say that I only had to take two manuscripts in with me to the meeting and not to forget to submit my website write up to her by 11pm. Fantastic.

Knowing she was gone for the afternoon was a huge relief, I relaxed in my chair and put some music on. I was lucky that I had literally walked into this job.

Laura had put a good word in for me and Jools was desperate as her last two assistants walked out after a month of being in the job. She was a pain in the butt, but she was good at her job and I was grateful for every working day.

Our office was situated on the third floor, there were lifts in the communal hallway, you turned left into our office, right for the toilets. As you entered through the glass doors, my desk was on the left, looking directly into the meeting room, which was on the right when you walked through the main doors. The meeting room was surrounded by glass, the back drop of the city was stunning. Jools's office was to my left, directly in front of the glass doors. It was only us and I was grateful at times.

I kicked my beautiful shoes off for a little while, they were Louboutin's. I had treated myself to them after my break up, to be honest, I deserved them. I had always wanted a pair but could never part with my money. They were very plain, black patent close toed shoe with the gorgeous red soles.

I looked at the time and realised it was nearly 1pm. I finished reading my second manuscript which I had started before lunch.

Two pm soon flew round. My desk phone rang, and I saw it was reception, "Hello, Freya speaking."

Our receptionist was called Rachel, she was lovely. She was only 22, her first job. "Hey," she whispered, "there is an extremely good-looking man in reception asking for you? He says he has a meeting with you at two pm, a Mr Cole?"

I laughed at her shyness and her trying to be discreet "Yup, that's right, send him up. Rach, if you aren't too busy, can you make me a coffee and ask Mr. Cole if he wants anything please?"

"Of course, see you in five."

I put the phone down, picked up my two chosen manuscripts, slipped my shoes on and walked into the meeting room.

I sat down, ran my hands over my skirt and turned my mobile on silent. I heard the office door go, Rachel had bought him up and showed him to the meeting room

"Freya, I will be back in a minute with your coffee."

I smiled, "Thank you Rachel. Mr. Cole, it's a pleasure to meet you, I'm Freya." I stood up, pulled my skirt down in the most discreet way I could and shook his hand.

"And it's a pleasure to meet you Freya, please, call me Carter," he purred.

Oh, his voice, he had a slight accent, but I couldn't quite work out where he was from. I had this feeling in the pit of my stomach when he said my name. I blushed. Pull yourself together Freya my subconscious snarled at me.

"Please, take a seat Carter." He undid his grey suit jacket button and sat down. He put his iPhone face down on the table. He was well built, very broad. His eyes were sage green, his hair was a mousy brown, he had slight freckles on his face and an amazing smile.

He smirked, "So, how did you feel when Jools asked you to cover for us?"

I cleared my throat, "I was a little surprised if I'm

honest."

He laughed. His voice was so easy to listen to, it was warm and just the right amount of deep. "Well, I asked her for someone who was hardworking, focused and was good at their job and she mentioned you!"

I was shocked, "Really?"

He looked confused. "Yes, really!"

I felt myself going red again. "I was wondering why you attended the meeting and not your Editor?"

He looked smug. "Because I can. I love reading, and I love finding new writers. Jools mentioned you had an aspiration to write, so I thought I would meet you personally to see if I can get a real feel for the manuscripts you have chosen." I just looked at him. He really was beautiful.

Rachel broke my stare. "Here we go, a coffee for you Freya, and a water for Mr. Cole."

"Please, Carter," he flashed her his amazing smile. Rachel also blushed a crimson red. She quickly rushed out the room and back in the lift.

We sat through the meeting making casual conversation while going through the manuscripts. One was a thriller type book that literally left me sitting on the edge of my seat, the other was a romance. My favourite. I looked at my phone to find it was already four-thirty.

As we finished our meeting, I stood up and so did he. He buttoned his suit jacket back up and shook my hand. He held on a little longer this time, then went to speak but didn't.

After what felt like forever, he finally spoke "I was wondering, can I take your number? Just easier so I don't have to go through reception or await a response by email."

I picked my phone up and smiled, "of course."

I walked him to the lift, holding the manuscripts to my chest. "Well it was lovely meeting you Carter, I will be sure Jools gets these manuscripts tonight. I already have put another three on her desk, so I am sure she will be in contact with you, again, it was lovely to meet you."

He took out his phone and pushed the button for the lift "You too Freya," my name slipped off his tongue so easily.

I tucked my hair behind my ear and smiled. He walked into the lift, pressed the ground floor button, "Goodbye, Freya," he gave me a grin as the lift doors closed.

My heart was thumping. I sat at my desk to gather my thoughts.

After five minutes, I placed the manuscripts on Jools's desk with a little post-it note.

I collected my bag, checked my phone, and realised I had missed a message from Ethan asking if tonight was still okay. I typed a quick reply and told him I was just leaving work and I would meet him in the little bar in the station. I shut my computer down, grabbed the office keys and locked our office. I stood in the elevator thinking the last couple of hours over in my head. I couldn't stop thinking about Carter. I rested my head on the walls of the lift, what a day. I walked out of the lift into reception and said bye to our security guard, Sid. I walked into the warm summer air and took a deep breath.

As I was walking to the station my phone beeped, I pulled it out of my bag and saw a message from an unknown number:

Hey, what a pleasure it was to meet you this afternoon.
Hopefully see you soon Freya.
Carter

I didn't text him back. I decided I would do it after I had met Ethan. I needed a clear head ready for our drink. I tossed my phone back into my bag and walked into the station. Even though Carter had completely knocked the wind out of my lungs, I was really looking forward to meeting up with Ethan.

I just made my train, so I sat down and closed my eyes for five 10 minutes. As we were pulling into Liverpool Street, I re-applied my lipstick, checked my phone to see if Ethan had text cancelling on me. Nope, nothing.

I got off the train and headed into the station. I walked towards the bar and could see him straight away, he was waving at me. His beautiful hazel eyes twinkling, his just perfect stubble and that gorgeous smile, with his slightly crooked teeth. I couldn't contain my smile.

"Hey you," he said and kissed me on my cheek.

"Hey," I replied. He had got me a glass of wine already,

perfect. This was the first time I had been on a date, obviously I met Jake in school so didn't ever really do the 'dating thing'.

We got lost in easy conversation, I laughed a lot. He was so lovely, and I didn't feel uncomfortable or awkward around him like I did with Carter.

I asked him where he lived, as he was describing his small block of flats, I realised he was describing my block.

"Wait, what? You live off of Highgate West Hill? In the renovated flats?"

He looked surprised, "yup, that's me. Have you been stalking me?" he raised his eyebrow.

"Nope, just I live there, have done for the last four months."

"No way! What a small world, how mad is that? I take it you are on the first floor then?"

"Yup that's me, and you must be on ground?"

He nodded "My 'sort of' friend Erin lives on the ground floor."

"Erin? Blonde hair? She is my next-door neighbour! How is Erin your 'sort of' friend?" he looked confused.

"Oh, she feeds Tilly the cat if I ever need her to, and to be honest, she is really lovely, and we do meet up for a cheeky glass of wine some evenings. She is always out and about with her flat mate Kirsten."

He smiled. "Is that the little red head one I always see her with then?"

I couldn't help but laugh, he was so dry, "yes, that's

Kirsten," I said laughing at him.

He laughed "I also know someone else in the flats, hence how I knew about the flat before it went onto the internet. My cousin Chris and his roommate Travis live on the first floor."

I blushed, "No way, are they together?" .

He gave me a look. "Er, nope, not that I know of – if they are they are good at disguising it with the number of women they bring home!" He ran his hand through his curly blonde hair and flashed me that smile.

After about an hour of us chatting, I found out he was in advertising. I explained my job to him which he seemed very interested in. I'm sure he was just being polite.

I looked at the time and realised I had to go. "Hey, I'm sorry to cut the evening short, but I need to get home as I have a deadline for 11pm, it's already nine and if I don't get it done my boss is going to kill me, I can't miss this opportunity."

He finished his beer, "it's fine, come on, let's go."

On our way home I found out, like me, he had just come out of a serious relationship. His was worse, he still has to work with his ex-girlfriend. He was 28 too, younger than me by three weeks.

We both walked to the block, all of a sudden, I realised I hadn't eaten since lunch time and I was so hungry.

We stopped off at our local chip shop because they smelled so good. I devoured them by the time I got home, and I then realised I wasn't alone. He must have thought I was a right pig.

As he walked me to my door, he put his arms round my waist. My tummy was fluttering, I felt him staring deep into my eyes. Before I could say anything, he kissed me, his soft lips caressing mine. Then he pulled away. "I had a really nice evening Freya, thank you."

I smiled up at him, "Me too."

I gave him a little kiss on the lips and let myself into my flat. I waved to him and watched him walk down the stairs. As he got to the corner of the landing on the stairs, he looked at me and winked. My stomach flipped. I closed the door smiling like an idiot.

CHAPTER SIX

I was still grinning like a Cheshire cat when I got indoors. I decided to get straight onto my email to Jools. It was 10pm, an hour to get it written and sent.

I looked at my phone and typed a quick reply to Carter. I text Ethan thanking him for a lovely evening, then locked my phone and placed it face down.

After fifteen minutes of nothing, I decided to go a grab a cold coke from the fridge. As I pondered, walking back to my room, my mind slipped to Carter. He was so mysterious but so hot. I doubt we would meet out of work, I'm sure he was just being polite, who knows. I sat back down at my computer and started to write.

Hey!

So, I have not long been home from my date. I met a very handsome man in a little shop near my flat. I assumed he was with a wife or girlfriend, he was just too good looking to be single.

Anyway, after talking for about fifteen minutes, I realised he was in fact single. Bonus. Now, I haven't had a date in, well, never.

That's a true story.

I was with my ex-boyfriend from the age of 16, he has been the only person I have been with. It feels weird writing that. I met Mr Hunk in Liverpool St straight from work. It was very easy to have a conversation with him, and I didn't even have to contact my best friend to get me out of my date. As we were talking, I found out he actually lives in my building and my friend is his neighbour. Small world ay!? Now I know he lives here, I might take myself over there every now and again for a glass of vino or two.

He gave me a little kiss on the cheek, my tummy started doing flips. It was nice having them feelings back again.

I've got my best friend's wedding in 6 weeks, I'm maid of honour. She has put me down for a plus one, obviously back then I was with my cheating ex, so he would and should have been coming with me, but he's not. Boo.

But now, I have this sexy man in my life, if things continue to go well, you never know, he could be my plus one. In fact, he could be THE one.

Woah slow down Freya, don't get ahead of yourself! Anyway, we will see. We haven't made any more dates, but I'm sure we will see each other again soon, I hope.

Love, Freya X

I had a quick read through and sent it to Jools with ten minutes to spare - get in. I took myself to the bathroom, jumped in the shower and got my pyjamas on.

I went out and locked the door, fed the cat and got a glass of water. As I got into bed I decided to check in with Brooke, I hadn't spoken to her for a couple of days. I then thought I would text Erin

Hey Doll, you didn't mention that a hot, blonde curly haired god moved next door to you?! & I thought me and Tilly cat meant something to you ;)!! Hope you are ok, let me know when you are free for wine xx

I looked at the time, 11:30, time for bed. I had a busy day tomorrow now I was doing two fulltime jobs and I really did need my beauty sleep in case I bumped into Ethan or Carter tomorrow.

I reached over and turned my lamp off, plugged my phone in to charge and started to get comfortable. Just as I was drifting into the land of nod, my phone beeped.

I debated leaving it, but worried, just in case it was an emergency. I rolled over with a huff and unlocked my phone. It was a message from Carter. My heart was racing. I opened the message and smiled as I read it.

I hope I didn't wake you, I just haven't been able to stop thinking about you. When are you free? I would love to take you out? Carter X

I typed a quick response, before putting my phone on silent and settling down for the night, it had finally hit me just how tired I was.

No, didn't wake me. I would like that, I'm free whenever. Now with this extra work I've been given, my social life is now extinct. You let me know when is good for you. Goodnight Mr. Cole, sweet dreams X

Oh, I will. Goodnight Ms. Greene X

I smiled, put my phone face down and snuggled into my duvet. As soon as my head hit the pillow, I was gone.

The next morning, I woke before my alarm, I debated whether to go back to sleep for another hour or so but decided against it. I got up, made a cup of tea and enjoyed the quietness of my little town.

I jumped in the shower then spent god knows how long debating on an outfit for work - I had to make sure I looked kind of decent in case Carter dropped in. I chose a black pencil dress with a round neck and capped sleeves. I ran my fingers through my knotty auburn hair, and threw it up in a semi-messy bun, pulled some stray bits out, applied a minimal amount of makeup and I might've gone a little over to the top with my perfume.

I was running early, so I enjoyed a cup of coffee in Starbucks before getting the dragon her order and going in for a chaotic day.

I walked passed Robert, our other security guard and wished him good morning. As I walked past the main reception, I gave Rachel a little wave and headed into the lift. I walked through and straight into Jools's office. I had been wondering whether she would mention anything about my email I sent her for the website.

"Morning, here's your tall black Americano," she looked up and smiled. I felt uneasy. "Thanks," she replied. I walked out of the office, not quite sure what to make of her mood. She rarely smiles, maybe she got some last night.

I logged on and opened my emails, there were 37 unread emails, most of them from CPH – mostly aspiring writers wondering if their manuscripts had been read. I scrolled aimlessly through when Jools shouted from her office. I nearly spilt my coffee down me. "Freya! Get in here please!"

I rushed into her office, "Yes, Jools?"

"Take a seat," she mumbled, I swallowed, hard. I sat down opposite her fiddling with my fingers. "I read your email, I liked it. I like the sound of this man, you are going to have to give him a nickname, so readers can imagine what he's like."

I nodded, "Okay, I can do that."

"Honestly, Freya. I really did enjoy reading it, but few things could have been better."

"Okay, no problem, is that all?"

She nodded, I got up and thanked her and started to walk out of her office. "Oh, Freya?"

I turned around, "Yes?"

Her smile crept back onto her face, "I heard Mr. Cole took quite a shining to you." I blushed, I tried to stop myself from blushing, but the more I tried, the more I felt it. "Well done on impressing him, I hear he's quite a hard man to break. He also agreed all five manuscripts you put on my desk last night. I have emailed Laura to send your payroll details over to his secretary so you can receive a small fund extra a month – oh, and please, go make me a normal coffee." Nothing could wipe this smile off my face; I was definitely meeting Laura for lunch today. I practically skipped out of her office and made her coffee.

I sat back down at my desk and sent a quick email to Laura arranging lunch again at the deli for 12:30. I couldn't wait to see her, nothing could bring me down from this high. I started on my first email and got lost in my work.

Lunch time soon arrived, this morning was flying. I left the office and met Laura at the deli. Once again, we were shown to our favourite table. Sometimes we liked to switch it up and swap seats, but that's about how far we would go. I sat facing out towards the restaurant, Laura faced the wall.

"So, missus, what is going on?" Laura asked taking a large mouthful of wine.

"Well, the dragon actually liked my blog and praised me!"

"That's fantastic babe! I am so proud of you, well done!" she held her glass up for a celebratory cheer.

"That's not it though..."

She looked up for her seafood pasta, "What else happened then?"

I smiled, "Mr. Cole agreed to publish the five manuscripts I chose! I am receiving a little bonus!"

She was beaming, "Oh Freya, that is fantastic, so that's why the dragon wanted me to forward your payroll details, well, again, well done I am super proud of you."

We carried on talking while I tucked into my delicious seafood pasta, then all of a sudden, my heart hit my stomach. *No way,* I thought. Laura saw from my facial expression that something was wrong "Sweetie, what is it?"

I just stared. I don't think I even blinked. "Jake has just walked in" I whispered, "with her."

Laura subtly looked over her shoulder, as she faced me I could see the horror on her face. "Let's go, come on." she said.

I came round from my stare "No! This is our local, our little hideaway, I'm not leaving." I saw Antonio look over and give me a puzzled look... he was just as baffled as we were. I necked the rest of my wine; it was like Antonio read my mind as he was over in a flash topping our glasses up.

What the hell was he doing here? What would make him come all this way? I looked down at my dinner, and tried to pick up conversation with Laura, when all of a sudden, I could feel eyes burning into me. I looked up and caught his stare. He tried giving me a smile. She wasn't at the table. I couldn't take my eyes off him. Laura by this point had turned to look at him as well. He quickly broke his stare when she walked back across the restaurant, she ran her hand across his hand which was on the table. I noticed she had a massive diamond ring on her finger "You've got to be kidding me," I muttered, "he's engaged?!" I was so angry.

"Freya, calm down, come on let's get the bill and go."

She got Antonio's attention and asked for the bill, he just shooed us away and mouthed he will cover it. She got up from the table, and came to my side, picking my bag up and taking my arm, "Come on sweetie, let's get out of here."

I was numb.

She walked me through the restaurant, as we got near their table I heard her mumble under her breathe, "Arsehole." as she walked past him.

As we got outside and the warm breeze hit me, I felt uneasy, "Oh god, Laura - I'm going to be sick."

CHAPTER SEVEN

After throwing up my delicious lunch that really didn't taste that great when it came back up, I just couldn't believe he was engaged. We always spoke about it, but it obviously never materialised, and what the bloody hell was he doing in London?!

I was sitting back at my desk, Laura asked me to promise to text her when I left work so she could get the train with me. I just wanted to sit on my own and process my thoughts, but she was just being the caring best friend that she was.

I didn't get that much work done that afternoon, my mind was playing the scenario over and over. What I wanted to say, what I could have said, but more importantly, what I didn't say. I logged off and turned the lights off to my office then I walked quietly towards the door. My week had been going great; now, now it'd taken a turn.

I met Laura in reception and smiled at her, "Hey you,

you ok?"

I raised my eyebrow, "Fantastic, hun," I said with a smirk.

"I'm sorry, I'm just not particularly good in these awkward situations."

I laughed and shook my head, "It's fine, promise."

She linked her arm through mine as we walked out of the office.

She was talking about her wedding and what still needed to be done for the big day. I had offered to help her, but she likes to do things alone, she is a control freak and I would just get in her way, but I still offer every time.

We just walked into the station when I heard a familiar voice call out "Freya...?"

Laura and I both turned around. It was him, standing there, like a little lost puppy.

Before I could do anything, Laura went storming over there "What do you want Jake?!"

He flinched as if she was going to hit him. "Laura, please, I just want to speak to Freya."

"Well she doesn't want to talk to you!" she hissed.

He looked round her, "Please Freya? Just talk to me."

I shuffled on my feet and twisted my fingers into knots, it felt like forever before I looked up at him, "Fine." I could feel Laura's eyes burning into me, "Laura, I will be five minutes, I promise."

I walked over to him, god I was sweating, hopefully he

wouldn't notice, "Well?"

He took my hand, I shuddered. All the feelings and memories came flooding back, "I'm sorry Freya. I know you will never forgive me, but please, I am sorry."

I pulled my hand from his "Is that it?" I was trying to sound harsh, but I couldn't.

"No, that's not it. I'm sorry you had to see me with her, we are in London because she has been offered a job here, so we are flat hunting and I'm being relocated."

I stopped him, "I don't want your life story Jake, if you've come here to gloat about your relationship then I'm not interested. I don't care." I did care, a lot. I don't want him knowing that I am single, with a cat and hardly any social life.

Yes, I've met two handsome men but that may go nowhere. He's winning this competition at the moment.

"No, no, sorry, I'm waffling, you know what I'm like when I'm nervous..." he gave me his cute half smile, "I can't stop thinking about you, I knew you were in London so, when I heard that we were coming here to flat hunt, well, I had to see you."

I just stared at him.

"Please Freya, I know it's a lot to take in, but I needed to tell you."

I shook my head and put my hand over my mouth, "I can't do this Jake... I've got to go." I brushed passed him and walked to Laura, "Please, can we go?" with tears in my eyes I carried on walking.

"Freya!" he called out, "Please!"

I wiped my eyes and got on my train, not looking back.

I sat at home in my scruffy pjs, my greasy hair thrown up in a bun, eating ice cream out of the tub while adding Amaretto to it and swigging big mouthfuls from the bottle. My eyes were puffy and raw from the nonstop crying. I couldn't stop thinking about this afternoon, how my morning had started off pretty perfect, and now it felt like a shit storm.

I turned my phone off and locked my door. I don't want anyone turning up, I can't be arsed to deal with them. I realised that I hadn't written my piece for the magazine.

I picked my laptop up and tapped my fingers on the mouse pad. Before I knew it, I just started writing and I couldn't stop.

Evening!

So, to be honest, the beginning of my week was going fantastic but unfortunately that has now taken a turn for the worse.

I was out for lunch with my friend at our local hangout when I noticed that my cheating ex was there with not only his girlfriend, but now his fiancée - I mean seriously?!

Why is he in my hangout! Why has he followed me? Haven't I been through enough to then have this rubbed in my face.

Do you know what he said to me? "I can't stop thinking

about you!" Oh really? You can't? That's a shame. Shame you weren't thinking of me when I caught you shagging her, and on my new rug may I add. What did you expect me to say to you? "Oh, okay then, let's go for dinner and talk this over." NO, I don't want to talk to you, I don't want you, I want to move on with my life.

I have dealt with the heartbreak and the crying over you, I am done. DONE. It's my turn for happiness, how dare you wait outside my work for me. Are you a stalker now?

Maybe you've realised what you have lost, well I'm sorry but it's too late. You lost me. I will never come back. It's OVER.

Now I am going to finish my massive tub of ice-cream and snuggle my cat because at least she loves me, well I think she does anyway, and binge out on TV shows. I don't want to think about you anymore tonight, I am over you.

Have a good night with your Fiancée if you read this. Oh, and if you do read this, don't contact me.

Douche Bag.

Love Freya X

I hit the keys to type in Jools's email address and sent it. I didn't even proof read it. I don't even think its 300 words. I slammed my mac lid down and threw it onto the chair opposite me.

I picked Tilly up off of the sofa and slumped myself down to cuddle her. I switched the TV on and put Friends on. Who did he think he was turning up and then telling me that he couldn't stop thinking about me?

Maybe he wanted to give it another shot, maybe he didn't want to marry Aimee – even the thought of her name left a sour taste in my mouth. She wasn't his type at all, but then again, they do say opposites attract. Maybe if we had both tried harder in our stagnant relationship, it would be me and Jake engaged, not them.

I groaned as I laid on my sofa, even Friends was making me depressed, it was the one where Rachel realises Ross is her Lobster. I love that episode normally, but not tonight – it just reminded me of how I was all alone. That's how it is going to be, me and Tilly. Forever.

I turned the TV off and went to bed. I debated putting my phone on, but to be honest, I don't want to deal with it. I got into my bed, buried my head under my duvet and shut off from the world.

I didn't sleep great that night. I looked at my clock, 5:30. I sighed, I decided to turn my phone on and deal with what came through. I dragged myself to the loo, tripping over my shoes on the way. I really should learn to pick my stuff up.

I scrambled back to bed, it felt brisk this morning. I checked my phone. I had a couple of messages from Laura, one from Brooke, she had obviously been filled in by Laura, three text messages from Jake and one from Carter. He had sent it last night when I was wallowing in self-pity. Pathetic, really.

Hey, how does this Friday work for dinner? I look forward to it.
    Carter X

I smiled but I didn't want to reply yet as it was too early. I made a mental note to reply to him on the way to work.

I flicked through my Facebook and Instagram - I really wasn't missing out on much. I flicked my laptop on and put Netflix on quietly in the back ground. I snuggled up and dozed back off.

My alarm went off waking me from a deep sleep. I stretched and looked at the time - 7am. I laid there for about five minutes. It was a grey miserable day outside. I pulled back the covers and headed for the shower.

As I was washing my hair, I remembered the email I had sent Jools. Panic set in, oh no, she's going to fire me. How could I be so stupid to write an angry article about Jake and send it to my boss to be published. I threw my head back and let the hot water course over my skin and face. What an idiot!

I rough dried my hair and applied some mascara and lipstick. My bags were awful. I went for high waisted suit trousers, a silk pink shirt and a cropped ¾ length sleeved jacket. I slipped into my faithful Louboutins and ran out of the door.

Whilst on the train I read my messages. The two from Laura were just to see if I was okay and that she would deal with Jake. I did laugh, she's so protective. Brooke's was a similar tone to Laura's. I typed a quick reply back to her to let her know I was okay.

I wasn't quite ready to read Jakes messages yet, maybe later. I then got to Carter's message and noticed he had sent me one this morning at 5:45am:

Freya, I didn't hear back from you? I hope you are ok, Carter X

Oh no, maybe I should have messaged him back this morning when I first woke up. I typed a quick message to him before pulling into the station.

Hey, you, Friday is perfect. Let me know details when you can. Sorry for the no reply last night, I switched my phone off, just needed some quiet time.
Freya X

I jumped off the train and headed up the stairs, I threw my phone into my bag - I really did need a new one - and put my mac on, it really had got quite cold. Typical British summer. I didn't stop at Starbucks today, no doubt the dragon would ask for another coffee as soon as I walked in with her Americano anyway.

I greeted Sid on the doors and gave Rachel a quick "Hi," then I got into the lift and took a deep breath.

Here we go, whatever happens, happens. I walked out of the lift and through the glass doors into our office. I hung my coat up on the coat rack behind my desk and threw my bag onto the floor.

I grabbed my phone out, silenced it and put it face down. I loaded up my computer and went through some of the paperwork while I was waiting for it to load. "Freya! Get in here, NOW!" Oh god. I slid back in my chair and walked into her office.

As soon as my foot stepped into her office, I could see how annoyed she was "Jools, I am so sorry!"

She looked at me, "For what?" she looked confused.

I blushed, "About my article I sent you last night, I had a bad night with an ex and unfortunately, I wasn't in the right mind set to write my website piece, but I was in the moment." I knotted my fingers together and looked at my feet. They really were gorgeous shoes.

"Freya, yes, the piece wasn't quite what I was expecting, but it was honest." I looked up at her, she actually had some compassion in her eyes, I had never seen that before - I didn't realise she had emotions.

I went to speak but she held her hand up indicating that she wasn't finished, "But, I can't publish this piece at the moment. You have written for us twice and you have already

66

had a meltdown after running into your ex. I am going to give you the rest of the week off from writing the article. You need time to find your peace with what has happened. If you need longer then let me know."

My face dropped, "but Jools..."

"No buts Freya, that's my final decision. Plus, Mr Cole seems very happy with you and would like to deal with you more often. He loved the manuscripts you chose. He sees potential in you Freya." I couldn't even speak, I was just staring at her. "Now, where's my coffee?"

I forgot her coffee. "Sorry, will do it now."

I ran into our little kitchen and made her coffee. I walked back into her office and placed it on her desk. She was engrossed in a phone call, as she looked at me I mouthed, "Thank you," she winked at me and then shooed me away.

I walked quietly out of her office and sat at my desk. I looked at my phone and noticed a message from Carter.

I can't wait, will send the details soon, Carter X

I unlocked my computer and went through my CPH emails and started printing the manuscripts. Today was going to be a busy one, and I couldn't wait to get stuck in.

CHAPTER EIGHT

The rest of the week went quite smoothly to be honest, but I was so glad it was Friday for two reasons.

One: because I was meeting Carter and Two: it was the weekend. I had my bridesmaid dress fitting Saturday morning which I was excited about. I clocked off early as I worked through my lunch.

I had arranged to meet Laura to go shopping in Oxford Street to find an outfit for tonight. Carter had been texting me all week, and not about work. He told me late Wednesday where we were going for dinner and that he would pick me up from my flat so we could drive together.

I said goodbye to Rachel and promised we would get an after-work drink some night next week. I had been texting Ethan through the week as I did really like him. He was trying to arrange another date with me, but I said I was busy and would get back to him with a date.

Laura met me in reception as we headed out onto a busy

Friday evening on Oxford Street. Carter had told me that we were going to The Ivy, in Convent Garden. I had never been but had heard excellent things about it. I didn't want to go to overdressed but didn't want to be to under-dressed either.

Laura reached for her bag and put her sunglasses on, the evening was still bright and warm. It felt good having the warm sun on my skin, "So, have you heard anymore from Jake?" she asked.

"A few messages here and there," I sighed, "why won't he just leave me alone?"

Laura shook her head, "I really don't know, hun. I don't understand why he is trying to get back into your head. It took you long enough to kind of get over him, why come back on the scene now?"

I didn't know why, I just shrugged my shoulders at her. We walked in silence for a little while looking around at the shop fronts, "So, are you excited for your dinner with Carter tonight?"

I smiled at the thought, "Yeah, I really am, it's kept me going this week knowing that I will be seeing him out of work – I was meant to have a meeting with him this week but he cancelled last minute due to a double booking in his diary. I did tell him to send the editor, but he refused, said he only wanted to deal with me and no one else."

Laura looked at me, "Oooh, he doesn't want anyone else dealing with you!" she winked at me and smirked.

I scoffed at her, "Not like that, honestly woman you

have such a filthy mind!"

She laughed, "well, I can't help it."

We stopped outside a little boutique shop. I loved these shops. You always find something a little different in them. As we walked in, the friendly assistant asked me if we needed any help. I smiled and said we were okay at the moment. I was lost in thought browsing through the dresses, "So have you prepared in case anything happens tonight between you two?"

"Laura!" my mouth dropped open, "sh, don't say that so loudly!"

She didn't see what she had done wrong, "What? It's just a question, have you? Just answer - yes or no."

I rolled my eyes at her, "Yes."

She squealed, "So you are hoping to get some then!"

"Oh my god, will you stop it! No, I am not hoping to get some, but I like to be prepared, I had a wax on Wednesday, I always book, and it just so happened it fell on this week."

She laughed "I'm calling bullshit, when was the last time you got that waxed?! You are a baby when it comes to that, there is no way you would put yourself through unnecessary pain if you didn't have to!" she raised her eyebrows at me.

"Oh shut up!" I snapped.

Just when I was about to give up looking, I came across a beautiful light floral midi dress. I called Laura over to the changing room. I pulled the curtain shut and started to get undressed. I really needed to get some nice underwear for tonight. I don't think my every day ones are going to cut it. "Laura, best place for nice underwear?" I could hear the smile on her face.

"Agent Provocateur – Selfridges, that's where I got my wedding lingerie from, their stuff is lovely," she said.

"And ridiculously expensive I bet," I mumbled to myself. I slipped into the midi dress. It felt so soft against my skin; it sat perfectly just off my shoulders and made my boobs look amazing. The right bra would do wonders in this dress, it sat nicely just under my knee and wasn't too tight if I was to sit down. My black Louboutin's definitely wouldn't look right with this dress, they would be too clumpy and harsh against the delicate floral printed onto it. I walked out of the changing room and Laura was buried in her phone "Come on, I need shoes."

£150.00 later we walked into Selfridges, I had managed to pick up a delicate silver strap sandal with a reasonable heel that matched the dress perfectly.

Laura was like an excited school girl helping me pick some underwear. We came to the top of the escalators and walked into the lingerie shop. She wasn't lying, their stuff looked amazing.

The dress was tight, so I needed some knickers that were not going to show through the material. There were so many types of underwear: thongs, laced, crotch less, suspender belts, high waisted and your typical cottons. I found a fine lace thong, the seam round the underwear wasn't thick, it was hardly noticeable. I looked over at Laura and she was talking to the assistant, most likely about her wedding underwear.

I headed over to the bras, I was so overwhelmed by the choice. I live in t-shirt bras, which to be honest, don't do much for my boobs, but they are so comfortable. I've never been one of those women that have fancy underwear. I decided on a strapless white, again, delicate bra. It had fine lace detailing and went with the thong I had picked up. Not that he was going to see me in this tonight, but I really did need underwear for this dress.

Another £200 down, Laura was throwing some more knickers and must have bras into my basket. She even picked me up a silk nighty in case we spent the night together. Honestly, did she think I was that easy? I have been with one man; I'm not going to hop into bed on my first date with Carter. As I thought about it that familiar burning sensation in my tummy came back, I thought about his beautiful sage eyes, his light freckles over his nose and cheeks, his dreamy, white perfect smile – my mind then drifted to his hands running down my body against the light silk night dress I had just picked up, his lips softly kissing my ears, slowly moving down to my neck, across my collar bone.

"Freya!"

I came around from my moment "Are you okay? I've been talking to you for the past five minutes and you have been standing there with this dumb look on your face."

I blushed. "I'm fine, was just thinking about dinner tonight."

She looked at me with a *yeah right* look, "Anyway, do you need any make up? I took the liberty of booking you in for a curly blow dry at the salon round the corner. I know how useless you are when it comes to your hair."

I smiled "No, no make-up, and thank you, that's nice of you".

We said our goodbyes and she made me promise to tell her everything tomorrow at brunch after our bridesmaid fittings.

I walked out of the salon and jumped into a taxi to take me to the station. As I walked into the apartments, Ethan was walking out of his door, "Look at you!" he said with a smile, his crooked teeth just showing.

I smiled at him; he really did have lovely eyes. "Thank you," I blushed.

"Where are you off to tonight then?" Oh shit.

"Oh, I have a date, what about you?"

His smile disappeared. "Oh nice, erm, I'm just heading out to the pub to meet my mates, I worked from home today so off to meet them. Have a nice time tonight."

He was blunt, he went to walk past me. "Hey, Ethan, don't be like that!"

He turned to look at me, "I'm not being like anything Freya. Speak to you soon."

I watched him walk out the apartment block. Why's he

being like that? We've only been on one date, if you could call it that.

I walked up the stairs and noticed a beautiful bouquet of a dozen white roses sitting outside my door. I picked them up and smelled them, they smelt so good.

I got my keys out of my bag and opened the door, Tilly ran past me and down the stairs. As I walked into my hallway, I threw my keys on the shelf next to the door and dropped my shopping bags down along with my tatty old bag. I placed the white roses on my kitchen counter and read the card:

I can't wait to see you, pick you up at eight. Carter X

I placed the card back in its holder and headed to the bedroom with a huge grin on my face. I hope he doesn't think he's coming back here tonight, my house was a tip. I started running a bath and pulled my hair up into a loose bun, so it didn't get wet.

I couldn't stop thinking about how Ethan had been when I bumped into him, it's not like we were exclusive, we had a couple of drinks after work. I shook the thoughts from my head. I needed to get ready for tonight. It was 6:45pm when I slid into the bath, it felt so good to just chill for a little while.

I got out of the bath and sat on my bed to do my make-up. I faced the window to get the best light. I never go overboard with make-up but thought I should go a little bit extra tonight. I applied a light layer of foundation, then a light dusting of bronzer and attempted to do a thin layer of liquid eyeliner on the top of my eyelid. I have green/grey eyes dependant on the light so wanted to make them stand out a bit.

After a quick YouTube video and four attempts, they didn't look too bad. I applied some mascara and applied a matt light pink lipstick I bought a few months ago. I moisturised my legs and re-painted my toes. I went to the hallway to get my bags, then dropped my towel and slipped into my new underwear. It felt nice against my skin.

I dropped my hair out of its messy bun and watched my thick auburn curls drop. They did a fantastic job of my normally dull, limp hair. I can curl it but only with tongs and it normally drops after a few hours.

I smiled as I looked at myself in the mirror, I actually felt good. I stood into my dress. Luckily, after being alone for quite a while I have learned how to do the zip up myself. The dress fitted perfectly, and not a trace of underwear could be seen. I put my delicate diamond earrings in that my parents bought me for my 21st. I really should call them tomorrow. I miss them. I slid my watch on and stepped into my new sandals.

After a quick spray of my Chanel No.5, I grabbed my silver clutch out the top of my wardrobe and put my lipstick, phone, debit cards, a small handful of notes that were in my big purse and keys in there. I shut my bedroom door, headed to the fridge and pulled out my bottle of Sauvignon Blanc.

I'm not very sophisticated when it comes to wine, as long as it is edible I will drink it. I poured myself a big glass, it was 7:45, early again. I was doing alright at this.

I was fidgety, one minute I sat down, then I was up pacing my living room floor looking out the window. I quickly ran to my bedroom and checked my make-up then I topped my lipstick up before finishing my glass of wine. I heard a knock at the door, oh god, he's here. "One second!" I shouted out, throwing all the odds and sods that were lying around and threw them into the bedroom. I really needed to start taking care of my house more; the cottage had always been tidy and spotless. I had just lost interest in making my lonely one bedroom flat look sparkling clean and tidy.

I checked my phone - bang on 8pm. I smiled at the photo of me and Laura on the background of us on her hen-do. I grabbed my clutch and opened the door.

My mouth dropped, oh he looked gorgeous, he smelled amazing. I had to hold onto the front door as I felt my legs buckle.

He was wearing a black suit jacket, and matching fitted in all the right places trousers with a crisp white shirt with the two top buttons undone. I could see his sun kissed skin, his broad shoulders looked relaxed and his eyes sparkled the most amazing green. My mouth went dry just looking at him. His mousy brown hair was tussled messy, and just the right length. He smiled at me, "Hello Freya, you look – I mean you've always looked beautiful when I've seen you, but you look amazing!"

I crossed my legs and looked down. I could feel the blush coming onto my face. I smiled at him, "Thank you for the beautiful flowers Carter." I looked over my shoulder and admired them.

"You are welcome, beautiful flowers for a beautiful woman – you ready?"

I nodded, stepped out the front door and locked it behind me. I thought Tilly would have been home, but she will go to Erin's if I'm not home.

We walked down the stairs together in silence; he held my hand as he opened the door to the apartments. Outside was a blacked-out car sitting at the pavement and a driver standing with the door open. "After you," he said. I thanked the driver and slid across the leather seats to make room for Carter. He gave me a kiss on the cheek and placed his hand on my leg. My heart skipped a beat at his touch. He made me so nervous. I could see his eyes looking me up and down as if they were undressing me. "A glass of Champagne?"

I nodded as he leant over and popped the chilled bottle of Dom Perignon 2006 from the cooler in the car.

"I'm looking forward to tonight," he said with a smirk on his face as he passed me the glass.

CHAPTER NINE

We arrived at the restaurant. As the car pulled up, Carter squeezed my hand. We had been having a brief conversation, mainly about work believe it or not, but he promised me that there would be no more work talk. The driver, who I have now worked out is called James, opened the door.

Carter did his suit jacket button up and stepped out of the car then turned and leant down to take my hand to help me out. "I will call you when we are finished James." James nodded at Carter then nodded at me. We walked up to the restaurant where there was a queue. Carter walked past the queue and straight up to the host on the door; his hand was resting on the small of my back. My skin burned every time he touched me.

"Evening Mr Cole, please follow me," he ushered me in front of him as he walked behind, "we have your usual table set and up and ready for you Sir."

As I looked around at the people in the restaurant, I felt out of place. *He obviously came here a lot for the staff to know him and the fact that he has a 'usual table.'* My trail of thought was cut short when the host arrived at our table. We were tucked out of the way, but near the bar and still close to see what was happening in the rest of the restaurant.

"After you, Freya, thank you Marius, that will be all."

Marius nodded and walked off into the hustle and bustle of the restaurant. Carter undid his jacket button once more as he took his seat opposite me. A friendly female waitress came over and asked what we would like to drink, all the time smiling at Carter. "We will take a bottle of the Condrieu please," he shut the menu up and handed it back to the waitress.

"Perfect," she said, still smiling at him, while he kept his eyes on me the whole time.

"How's your day been?" he asked, I looked back up at the waitress as she poured the white wine then looked back at Carter.

"It wasn't too bad to be honest, being kept busy by certain people," I said with a smirk, "but I did get to leave early as I worked my lunch so I could head to the shops."

He took a mouthful of the wine, I mirrored him. Oh, it was good.

He placed his glass down, "Well you tell whoever is keeping you busy to back off," he said with a smile, "what did you buy? Something new for tonight?" he teased.

"I did actually yes, everything I am wearing is new, thought I would treat myself."

He tilted his head and looked at me, then my dress "Well, I must admit you chose very well, you look breath taking." I smiled at him. He was a charmer.

"So, tell me about you, Mr Cole," I said as I tucked into my seabass. The food was amazing.

I was still drinking the white wine Carter had ordered but he had moved on to a Santenay to compliment his steak. He looked up from his dinner, "I like it when you call me by my last name Ms. Greene – what would you like to know?"

I put my knife and fork down and topped my wine up, "Where are you from? I can't help but hear that little twang when you talk?"

He laughed a belly laugh. "That twang Ms. Greene is Australian. I'm originally from a town called Evandale, which is in Adelaide."

I wasn't expecting that, I thought he might have come out with Liverpool or something. "Wow, Australia, I've never been but would love to visit. What made you move to London?"

He took a mouthful of his red wine and shuffled in his seat. "We moved to London when I was eighteen, my father wanted to expand Cole Enterprises over to the UK after buying a few struggling firms here, mainly shipping yards and boat manufacturers, so we followed him. I still go back from time to time to make sure our company is a success back in Adelaide, but I'm mainly here. I have an apartment over there, and my parents' house is still there, they didn't want to sell it." He cleared his throat, "My mum likes to go back over there, but she doesn't like travelling alone so she normally waits for my sister to visit then flies back with her. My sister, Ava, heads up our business back home, but both are solely owned by me, being the first born and only son, my father passed the companies over to me when he was taken ill," he shuffled in his seat.

"Oh, Carter, I'm sorry."

He took my hand, "It's okay it was nine years ago now when he passed."

All of a sudden, I felt sorry for him, I take my parents for granted every day and I still haven't called them this week. I needed to do that tomorrow.

He let go of my hand and continued to eat, "Now tell me about you, what's your life story?"

I took another bite of my sea bass, "Well, there isn't much to know. I am originally from Elsworth, Cambridgeshire where I worked for a family law firm, and then I decided to move to London after being offered a job at You Magazine."

He looked at me as if he didn't believe me, "Why would you just decide one day to move from your hometown to London?"

He smirked at me, I put my hair behind my ear, "Well, I just wanted to move away, become independent."

He laughed, "I'm not buying it. Who were you running from?"

I rolled my eyes, "An ex. It was hardly running, I caught him cheating, my best friend lived here and managed to get me a job at You Magazine, so I really had nothing to stay for." I felt a pang of nerves bolt through my stomach.

He looked puzzled, "Why on earth would anyone cheat on you?"

I shrugged, now holding onto the stem of my wine glass, "He had his reasons obviously. He's now engaged and moving to London because she's been offered a job here."

I let out a big breath, I looked up and caught his eyes, "He is an idiot, but his loss is my gain." He smirked.

"Anyway, let's move away from my life and back to yours."

He shook his head "Nope, let's not talk about our lives anymore, do you fancy getting out of here? We can go back to my place for a drink?"

I knew what that meant, a drink – sex. "I'm not sure. I have a bridesmaid fitting tomorrow, early."

He stopped me. "I promise, just one drink – that's it?"

I checked my phone, eleven pm, "okay, one drink."

As Carter was signalling the waitress over to get the bill, two girls walked by our table to go to the bar - one tall, beautiful blonde-haired sex goddess looked at Carter. "Carter," she purred as she walked, he looked at her and smiled.

"Evening," he replied.

She turned around and mouthed "Call me."

I couldn't help staring at her, she had a bandage mini dress on which stuck to her body in all the right places, her legs were tanned and long - she was beautiful. I was now feeling uncomfortable. *Maybe I should just go home,* I thought. Carter could obviously read my body language "Hey, you have nothing to worry about, she's just" he paused "– some girl."

I just nodded. It was none of my business what she was, so why was I getting so jealous? The waitress appeared with our bill, with the same stupid smile on her face. I mean I can understand it, he really is gorgeous. I reached into my clutch to get my card and he just shook his head at me, "I don't think so, gentleman don't let their ladies pay." My heart thumped. 'Their ladies.' Did he see me as 'his lady'? He stepped out of the table and took my hand, "Come on beautiful, I've called James, he will be out front in five."

As we waited outside, he placed his suit jacket round my shoulders, and nuzzled his face into my hair. I was so content just standing there watching the world go by.

Like clockwork, James pulled up to the kerb; he took my hand and walked me to the car. I took his jacket off and placed it over my lap. Carter was sitting himself next to me, but he was leaning against the door, so he was facing me. He had a smouldering look about him.

He ran his thumb across his bottom lip and patted the

seat for me to move closer to him. The nerves kicked in, I felt like I was sweating. *Please oh please do not let me have sweat patches.* I moved over and sat next to him, he placed his hand back on my leg like he did on the way to the restaurant.

He moved his hand slowly up to my face and tucked a loose curl behind my ear. I felt like I had stopped breathing. He ran his hand down my face and slowly run his thumb across my lip, "I want to kiss you," he whispered.

I felt a shiver run through my body and before I could register what he had said I replied, "Kiss me then."

He cupped his hand around the back of my head and pulled me towards him. His lips touched mine as he softly kissed me. I felt like I had electricity coursing through my body. His other hand was still firmly on my thigh as he moved it down and run it across the hem of my dress. A dull ache hit me deep in my body. Our kiss got more intense as he slowly introduced his tongue, it wasn't too much – intense, but a nice intense. His hand slowly started making its way up my dress, but I panicked and pulled away.

Trying to catch my breath, "Slowly, take it slow," I whispered. I steadied my breath and knotted my fingers, "Sorry," I mumbled.

He cupped my chin and tilted my head to look at him, "Don't say sorry, I've wanted to do that from the moment I stepped into your office – do you know how many times I have had to stop myself coming over to your office this week and making a move on you?" he was getting worked up, "You are a wonderful woman Freya, a woman I want to get to know better. Please come back for a drink."

I thought about it, I really wanted to, but I kept playing scenarios out in my head, it would end up being a one night stand and having to work with him would be awful. I started thinking out loud "I shouldn't, because I know what will happen, I will come back... we will have a drink and then..." I looked at him.

"And then what?" he asked.

"And then we would end up sleeping together and then that would make work awkward as you wouldn't want to know me anymore."

I turned to look out of the window. I heard him exhale deeply, "Why would you think that? I like you Freya."

I placed my hand on his, "One step at a time Carter."

He leant over and kissed me on the forehead, "Okay, if that's what you want."

Before I knew it, we pulled up outside my apartment block. James came around and opened the door and Carter followed me out "Honestly, stay in the car, I'll be okay." I turned to James, "Thank you," he nodded and smiled.

As I walked up the stairs, Carter followed me "Let me at least see you into your apartment?"

I nodded.

We walked up the stairs in silence, I got my keys out of my bag and put them in the door, "Thank you Carter for a wonderful night."

He put his hand on my hip, "You are most welcome Freya, sleep tight." He leant in and gave me a kiss goodnight – he really was a good kisser.

"Goodnight Carter."

I let myself into the apartment and watched him walk down the stairs as I closed the door. I smiled as I looked at the roses Carter had sent this evening, they were beautiful.

I threw my clutch down and slipped my shoes off, my feet were hurting so bad. I unzipped my dress and let it fall to the floor. I pulled my hair up into a messy bun then grabbed my clean Guns N Roses t-shirt, it was an XL, but I only bought it for bed. I threw it on, then headed to the fridge to get myself a glass of wine when I heard a knock at the door. *It must be Erin bringing Tilly back*, I thought. I swung open the door to see Carter.

Oh shit.

"Carter wh..." I couldn't say anymore, he picked me up and wrapped my legs around his waist, our mouths finding each other. I wrapped my arms around his neck and pulled on his nape of neck before running my hands up and pulling on his messy hair.

He slammed the door shut and carried me into the living room. He broke his kiss as he looked around, "Please, don't look it's a mess." I was so embarrassed, *mental note Freya, make sure the house is always tidy.*

He smiled and carried on kissing me. He sat down on

the sofa, so I was now sitting on his lap. He didn't let me go so I moved my hands round to his face and ran them along his jaw line. His hands moved from round my waist and ran under my t-shirt as he placed his warm hands on my hips. He moved from my lips, down to my neck, "stop" I said catching my breath. He looked up at me with so much hunger in his eyes, "Why did you come back?"

He sat back on my sofa and looked at me, "I didn't want to go home without you."

He moved closer to me, I could feel his warm breath on my face, I bit my lip "I'm not very good at this, you know, so..."

He put his finger on my lip "I don't believe you."

I moved his finger away and dropped his hand to my lap, "Why do you think my ex cheated on me?"

He looked seriously at me, "Because he's an idiot."

I shook my head, "I've never slept with anyone else, we didn't really do this... it was scheduled for certain nights and certain times."

Carter smirked up and me while slowly lifting my t-shirt, he gave a subtle smile when he saw my knickers I was wearing. "He's even more of an idiot now," he said in a husky voice as he continued kissing my neck. His kisses traced down to my collar bone while his fingers explored my body.

He slowly moved his hands down around my bum, I felt him grow underneath me. He then slowly moved his hands from my bum and round to my knickers. His fingers caressed in-between my thighs, it felt so good. He carried on this slow rhythm which was building me up, he looked at me, mouth slightly open as his breathing fastened, he then covered my mouth, kissing me, his tongue slowly animating his finger movements. I could feel myself building higher. I didn't want it to stop.

He stopped for a brief moment and moved my knickers to the side, exposing me. His fingers finding their place, he slowly entered his finger inside me "Mmm..." he growled from his throat, "You feel so good..." I was so lost in him, in the moment. My hips were moving to his rhythm as he continued to slowly slide his finger in and out. He came up to my ear and whispered, "You are driving me wild, I can't wait to fuck you." The words made me shudder. He pulled his finger out slowly and pulled my knickers back over.

He slowly lifted me up and went over to his suit jacket which was thrown on the chair. He reached in his inside pocket and pulled out a condom.

"Come," he said softly and held his hand out. I took it, still feeling lost in the moment. He walked me through to my bedroom and cleared the bed. I didn't care how messy my room was, my stomach was in knots and burning, I needed this man, now.

CHAPTER TEN

We stood at the foot of my bed, I looked up at him. I never realised how tall he was, he must be about six, five. I leant up and kissed him, his hands were resting on my hips. I slowly ran my hands down his chest and started undoing his buttons, as I got to the bottom one, I took a step back from him so I could admire him.

He was beautiful, his sun kissed skin glowing, his toned stomach and his dark snail trail was perfectly trimmed. I ran my finger down from his chest, then slowly down his snail trail and along his belt. He grabbed my hand and shook his head. He picked me up and laid me on the bed. "Tonight's about you," he smiled.

My insides were squirming; I was nervous and excited at the same time. He pushed my legs apart and admired the view, then he moved up towards me and started kissing me. His hand ran back down to my sweet spot but this time he was more forceful. He stopped and unbelted his trousers and slid them off, next thing to go were his pants. I propped myself up on my elbows to marvel at him. His shaft sprung from his pants, it was thick, so thick. I swallowed hard. He slowly slid the condom down his penis and looked up at me. Then, he pulled me up and removed my t-shirt.

"I like your underwear, Freya, it seems a shame to remove it."

I blushed.

He unclipped my bra, slowly sliding it down my arms, then he pulled my thong down my thighs and slowly off my feet.

He then moved in-between my legs and slowly inserted his finger back inside me. I could feel how aroused I was by him. I groaned as he did it again, following his movement. "Are you ready?"

I nodded; I was hungry for him now. He slowly removed his finger and slid himself inside me. He took my breath away, literally.

I could feel him moving so slowly at first and it felt so good. He was looking down at me, our eyes meeting. He started to pick up the pace, he cupped my boob into his hand and started slowly flicking my nipple with his tongue, the feeling of that and him inside me was driving me wild.

I looked down to watch him moving in and out of me, it was such a turn on. I started to tense up, I could feel myself brimming, "Carter," I whispered, he looked up at me smirking, "I'm going to come." With that, he started moving faster. The build-up was so intense, I felt myself go as my back arched as my orgasm hit my body. My whole body was tingling as Carter finished.

He lay next to me panting then leant up on his side and kissed me gently, "You were amazing." I pulled my duvet up to my face to hide. "Hey, don't hide," he pulled the duvet down and looked at me.

"I'm going to the bathroom," I whispered. I sat up and looked for my t-shirt, it was hanging on my bedside table. I picked it up and put it on and walked to the bathroom.

I stood in front of the mirror, I felt like a new woman. Is that what I've been missing? I don't ever remember sex being like that with Jake.

I ran my fingers over my lips and down my neck. My skin was on fire. I freshened up and went back out to the bedroom. "Hey…" as I looked Carter was asleep. I stood and watched him for a minute or so then walked out to the hallway and locked the front door. I heard meowing so I quietly opened the door and let Tilly in.

I tiptoed back to my bedroom, shut the door and crept into bed. I felt exhausted.

I woke up with a jolt, I rolled over to see Carter spooning me, I can't remember when I was last spooned, it had been so long since I've had someone in my bed. I'm not used to it. I stretched over and reached for my phone. 3:30am. I looked at Carter again, his long eyelashes, his perfect even freckles, his mousy brown hair messed up. He looks so peaceful. I snuggled back down into bed and nuzzled into my duvet.

I was awoken by a noise in the kitchen. I sat up and saw Carter was out of bed. It was 7am. I walked out into the living room to see he was making tea, "Hey you," I said as I stood leant up against the bedroom door frame.

He turned with a beaming smile, "Good morning, how did you sleep? Sugar?"

He had his boxers on, my mind started running back to last night, "I slept very well Mr Cole, what about you? And no, thank you."

He passed me my cup of tea and kissed me on the lips, "Best sleep I've had in ages." He walked into the bedroom as I watched him over my shoulder. He was so hot. "Okay to jump in the shower?" I nodded while taking a mouthful of tea.

I sat on the bed browsing through my phone. I had a message from Laura asking me not to be late and to meet her straight at the bridal shop for 10:30am.

I made the bed and looked through my wardrobe for something to wear. I pulled out some black skinny jeans, a light grey crew neck t-shirt and my havaianas flip flops. I even decided to wear some more of my new underwear.

The sun was beaming through the window, today was going to be a good day. Carter emerged from the bathroom and then started looking for his clothes. I pointed over to my chest of drawers, I had folded them up and placed them there. "Thank you," he said as he grabbed them.

"I'm going to get in the shower, I need to be with Laura for 10:30, the train journey is going to take 45 minutes."

He walked over to me, "I will drive you," he said, I looked at him.

"Oh, so you do drive then?" I said with a smirk.

"Yes Freya, I do drive." Ohh he could be so serious.

"Okay, well I'm going to jump in the shower and get ready, I won't be long. There's bread in the cupboard or cereal, help yourself."

I walked into the bathroom and ran the shower, I took my top off and let the hot water burn my skin, it felt so good. As I washed myself, I remembered the details from last night, his kisses down my neck and collar bone, his fingertips running over my body then slowly touching me in my sweet spot. It was amazing.

I stepped out, wrapped my towel and let my messy bun down. Amazing, the curls were still there, and my hair still looked fresh. I brushed my teeth and stepped back into my bedroom. Carter was dressed and, on his phone, typing an email by the looks of it.

I walked over to my clothes and stepped into my underwear, Carter looked over and shook his head. He undid my towel and dropped it to the floor. "I want to look at you, it was dark last night so I didn't get to enjoy the view." I went crimson red. "Freya, don't be embarrassed, you have a very sexy body," he stood over me and put his hands round my waist, "You should come to work like this, I could look at you all day – but then I don't know how much work we would get done."

I laughed at him, "I don't think Jools would be very happy..."

He clocked his head "When is she ever happy?"

"That is true," he came in and gave me a kiss; his kisses were good.

I peeled his arms from around my waist, "I really need to get ready; you don't know Laura, she can't stand it when people are late, and apparently, I am always late." I slipped my silk knickers on and matching bra, it's amazing what a good bra can do for your boobs. I shimmied into my skinny jeans and threw my crew neck top on. Then, I applied a bit of bronzer and lip gloss and put my flip flops on. I picked my phone up and text my mum.

Hey mum, hope you and Dad are ok. Just off for my bridesmaid fitting, will call you later, Love you xx

I felt sad, sad for Carter. I couldn't imagine a life without my mum and dad.

"Come on handsome, we've got to go," I said as I walked down the hallway.

"Right behind you baby," he said. I picked my tatty bag up and sighed, I really do need to get myself a new bag.

Carter went out first and waited on the landing while I

locked the door. We walked down the stairs and there at the bottom by the communal letter boxes was Ethan. Shit. Here I am standing with Carter. *Fuck, fuck fuck, what do I do?* before I could run back up the stairs, he saw me.

"Hey Freya," Carter's grip tightened around my hand.

"Hey Ethan! How are you? Did you have a nice night?"

His hazel eyes glistened as he looked up at me. "Yea I'm fine, it was good, take it yours went well as well then?"

I tried to pull my hand out of Carter's, but he wouldn't let me, I looked at him but he was just staring at Ethan. "Erm, yeah it did…" I mumbled. I could tell Ethan was pissed off,

"Good." he replied bluntly.

We stood there in an awkward silence for a minute or two, "Anyway, I've got to run, bridesmaid dress fitting…"

Carter still staring at Ethan, Ethan staring at Carter. "Yeah cool, will text you later," with that Ethan walked towards his apartment.

Finally, my heartbeat slowed down; Carter was still holding my hand a bit too tight. We got outside the apartments and a car was sitting outside front, I assumed it was Carter's. It was a Maserati Alfieri in charcoal grey. How much money did the man have? He opened the passenger door, not once looking at me.

I slid in uncomfortable by his mood. He slammed the door and then got into the driver's side. "What's wrong with you?" I asked puzzled.

"Nothing, I just didn't like the way he was looking at

you, like you were his property or something."

I scoffed, "I am no one's property, Ethan is my friend, a good friend."

I saw his grip tighten on the steering wheel, "Do you like him like that?"

Jeez, what was with the questions? "I do like him, yes." *Not that it's any of your business psycho.*

"Have you been on a date with him?"

I rolled my eyes. "Yes, we went for drinks after work last week. He's new to the building and the area."

Carter frowned, he looked at me while we were at traffic lights, "I don't want you seeing anyone else."

What?! "Are you joking?"

His eyes were back on the road. "No, Freya, I am not joking. I don't want anyone else near you apart from me."

I shook my head, "Pull over, I want to get out."

He looked at me, "What?"

I was angry now, "You heard me, pull over. I'm not having you tell me what to do, in work I have to listen to you, you are technically my boss, but out of work I don't have to, so pull over."

He pulled up to the kerb, "Freya, please don't do this."

I opened the door, "I didn't do anything Carter, you did!" I slammed the door and walked onto the pavement.

He drove slowly next to me, "Freya, please get back in the car, I'm sorry."

I stopped and looked at him "I am no one's property

Carter, not yours, not Ethan's, so don't think you own me because you don't!"

He stopped the car and looked down at his lap like a naughty schoolboy who had just been scolded.

I walked back round to the car, as I got in and sat down he took my right hand, "Freya, I'm sorry, I just get protective and I like you." He kissed my hand and pulled away from the kerb. I didn't say anything, I had nothing to say at that moment. I was too busy festering on what had just happened.

I pulled my cheap sunglasses out of my tatty bag and put them on, not saying anything for the duration of the journey. Carter had put his music on to drown out the silence.

I smiled inside as he played some classic Luther Vandross, I love Luther.

CHAPTER ELEVEN

Carter dropped me outside the bridal boutique, I checked the time on my watch 10:27. I didn't look at him as I got out the car. I walked round the back and onto the pavement, he had put his window down, "I'm sorry, baby."

I put my sunglasses on the top of my head, "Thank you for the lift, loved Luther by the way." I turned away and walked into the boutique.

I pushed the heavy door into the beautiful bridal shop, stunning gowns were everywhere, champagne wallpaper from floor to ceiling, and big ornate gold mirrors hung on most of the walls. It really was a gorgeous shop.

I could see Laura with Brooke and Zoe, "Hey girls," I said as I walked up behind them. How the hell was I the last one there?

"Hey doll," Laura said as she greeted me with a kiss on the cheek whilst Brooke and Zoe gave me a wave.

The shop assistant came out to us, "Hey ladies, so we

are all here, let's go and try the dresses on."

We were walked through to the dressing room. The curtains on the four changing rooms were heavy cream crushed velvet, the walls the same champagne delicate wall paper. We were shown to our dressing rooms where our dresses were hanging up. *I bloody hope it fits,* I thought. They were chiffon material, sweet heart neck in a subtle champagne colour with slight sequin details round the neckline.

I heard Wendy, the assistant, tell Laura she would be back in ten minutes. I unzipped the dress, it was lovely. "Freya, are you going to fill us in on your date?"

I was so glad I was behind the curtain. "Yeah it was good, we ate, drunk and talked," I laughed to myself.

If she thinks I'm indulging what actually happened last night she can forget it, "Anything else happen?"

"No Laura, drop it," I stepped into the dress and pulled it over my thighs and bum. I had to have a little wiggle to get it up then pulled it up around my boobs.

I looked at myself in the mirror and smiled, it was fitted right down to the waist, it then came out ever so slightly and fell to the ground. I pulled back the curtain and asked if Laura could do my zip up. I moved my hair to the side as she slid the zip up. It got a bit stuck halfway up but after a bit of fiddling she managed to get it done up to the top. "Well, what do you think?"

Laura held her hands under her chin and just smiled,

"Oh, they are so lovely!"

Brooke and Zoe then emerged, here we were, her three bridesmaids. A little while later Wendy re-appeared "Okay, let's check these and see if any changes need to be made." she smiled at us all.

After what felt like forever, we were all measured up and good to take the dresses off. Zoe needed hers taken in slightly, mine needed to be taken up and Brookes fitted perfectly.

Laura made an appointment to come and pick the dresses up in three weeks' time. We walked outside the bridal boutique and I checked my phone, three messages from Carter and two missed calls.

I pulled my sunglasses down and threw my phone back in my bag, I would deal with him later.

We walked a short way until we came to a little restaurant. We were seated in a booth at the back of the restaurant. When the waiter came over and asked what we wanted to drink, Laura piped up and ordered a bottle of prosecco and four glasses. The waiter jotted it down and left us with some menus.

"I'm starving, I haven't eaten since last night," I moaned, the girls eyeballed me.

"That's unlike you, you never normally skip a meal," Laura said looking at me.

"Well I wasn't very hungry this morning, and I do sometimes skip meals, if I'm busy, or sick..." she rolled her eyes at me.

I decided on a steak salad, Laura went for a prawn salad, Brooke a chicken pasta and Zoe a steak sandwich with chips. As our lunch arrived and we were on to our third bottle of prosecco, I started to give in on what happened last night. As I started talking they all sat like excited school children. "So, when I come home from shopping with Laura, I found a bunch of white roses outside my front door."

They all "Ahhhh'd" in perfect harmony.

"Anyway, I got dressed and Carter was at my door bang on 8pm, he showed me to our car and then he took me to The Ivy. We had nice food and good wine and we learned a lot about each other," I said, shoving some lettuce leaves into my mouth. Thank god, he wasn't here now, as much as he has annoyed me, I miss him.

"Then what?" said Brooke with her prosecco in her hand, food barely touched.

"Then we got back into the car and he sat opposite me, not next me to this time," I took a swig of my prosecco, "he sat giving me these smouldering eyes, then he asked me to sit next to him, not going to lie I was so nervous..." I started tapping nervously on the table.

I started having flashbacks from the night before, his smell, his kiss, his touch, I looked up and all three girls were just gawking at me "Sorry – got a bit side tracked. So, he kissed me, but it wasn't just a kiss, it was a steamy, hot, amazing kiss and yeah, I said I wasn't going back to his. I had already got indoors and undressed and there was a knock at my door and low and behold it was Carter, I didn't get the chance to ask him what he was doing here as he scooped me up and well, we went on to have the most amazing sex."

Laura's mouth dropped open, Brooke didn't know what to say and Zoe was just staring at me.

"What?" I asked them, confused on why they were staring at me like they were.

Laura cleared her throat "Oh my god, you actually slept with him on the first date?!"

I swallowed a big mouthful of prosecco and replied, "Erm yeah, it wasn't planned, and like I said, I did go home. It was just in the moment..." They fell silent, while they were processing this new Freya. I sat smugly, picked up my fork and carried on eating my lunch.

After a lot of laughing and indulging into the details of last night we settled the bills and said our goodbyes. I jumped in a taxi to get home, I didn't fancy the train today - it was too stuffy. I pulled my phone out and read Carter's messages.

Hey, I am really sorry about earlier, come over to my place tonight and I will make it up to you, Carter X

Freya, please answer me, I will send a car for 7:30pm, See you soon X

I typed a reply, I had ignored him all day and I did feel a bit bad.

See you at 7:30pm, looking forward to talking X

I was blunt with him, but I needed time to think it over. I walked in the door and said hello to Tilly, I had missed this little cat of mine.

I sat on the sofa and looked around, reliving the moments with Carter last night. I put the cat down next to me and decided to ring my mum and dad.

After a 45-minute conversation promising them I would go to see them in the coming weeks I said my goodbyes. It was 5pm, I decided to have a long soak in the bath. I laid there for a good twenty minutes before doing anything. I wanted to wear something that he wasn't going to be able to resist me in, just to be a tease. I washed my hair then hopped out the bath.

I really did need to speak to Ethan. Maybe I could do that tomorrow morning once I've sorted this with Carter.

I sat on my bed and pulled out my faithful mirror that I've had since I was a teenager and propped it up against my bedside table. I applied some concealer under my eyes, even though I slept well they looked dark. I then did a light dusting of bronzer and put my mascara on. I dried my hair and ran the straighteners over the ends.

I walked over to my wardrobe and picked out a white t-shirt dress with a lace up corset at the front, just for show obviously, sported with my flip flops. I chose another new under wear set, this time a full lace basket bra and matching thong; I sighed at the price tags, but they really were amazing. I took a look in the mirror for one final check, the t-shirt dress was a bit see through, that should get him riled up. I couldn't help it. I'd never been like this before.

I fed the cat and waited for the knock on the door, if James actually knocked, he may call. I put my phone on loud. No messages from Carter confirming our date, but no cancellation either. I hadn't heard from Ethan, but to be fair after this morning I doubt I would. I opened my messages and typed

Hey, I'm sorry about earlier, are you free tomorrow for a coffee? I don't want it to be awkward between us. Freya X

Hopefully he will take me up on my offer, I like him and don't want to ruin anything because of this morning's shenanigans.

I looked at the time, 7:34pm, he was late.

All of a sudden, I heard a light knock on the door, I grabbed my bag and my keys and walked to the door. It wasn't James, it wasn't Carter, it was Ethan.

What the hell was he doing here? "I should have done

this last Friday," he muttered then he came through the door and clasped his hands around my face. His kiss was different to Carter's, it was hard, forceful.

I pulled away, "Ethan! What are you doing!?" I yelled.

"Oh, so it's okay for Mr Suit to do it, but I can't?" he shouted. He was out of breath and clearly annoyed.

"Who says me and 'Mr Suit' as you called him did anything?" I furrowed my brow.

He rolled his eyes at me "I'm not fucking stupid Freya!" he barged past me and into my living room pacing up and down. "What's he got that I haven't then? There must be something because I thought we had something good, I felt something last Friday, didn't you?"

I knotted my fingers.

"Well, didn't you?" he shouted.

"I, I did..." I stammered. I didn't like this side of Ethan, it made me uneasy, I feared this side of him.

"Give me a chance, don't settle for him," he said in a quieter tone.

I looked at him, "I'm not settling for anyone, I have been on one date with you, and one with Carter! Who do you both think you are?" Ethan looked up at me dumbfounded, "I decide who I want to see, who I want to hang around with!" I could feel myself getting worked up "It's not down to anyone else!"

I picked my bag up that had been knocked to the floor "I want you to leave." I said abruptly.

Ethan walked towards me, I could tell by his eyes that he was upset with himself, "Freya, I.." he stood in front of me and kissed me on the lips, but it was like he was hardly touching them, "I'm sorry, I just, I can't even explain what was going through my head..." he still stood there, as if he couldn't move.

"Ethan, I want you to leave, please," I looked down at my feet.

He just stood there in front of me with his hand resting on the wall, I looked back up at him when I heard a familiar voice, "she told you to leave." I looked round at the front door and there stood Carter.

They locked eyes with each other for what felt forever then Ethan finally broke contact and looked back down at me. He apologised once more and walked out.

"Are you okay?" Carter whispered as he came to my side and ran the back of his right hand along my cheek bone.

"I'm fine, he just wanted to talk about earlier, and he was upset."

Carter just nodded, "Come on, lock up, the cars outside." He kissed my forehead.

I checked to make sure I had everything in my bag and walked out of the flat locking the door behind me. He took my hand and lead me to the car. James was there holding the door open, "Evening James," I smiled at him as I stepped into the car.

Carter sat next to me and ran his thumb across my

knuckles, "You look wonderful Freya."

My eyes lit up, "What in this old thing?" I laughed, "You don't look too bad yourself." It was weird seeing Carter dressed causal. He was wearing a loose khaki crew neck t-shirt and black skinny fitting jeans with black converse. He smelt amazing as per usual.

We sat in silence as I took the city lights in, London really is beautiful when you sit quietly and watch.

I was distracted when I felt Carter move as he leant down and pulled a box out from under his seat, "This is a little gift for you, a sorry present for being a jerk." I stared at the box not quite believing what I saw. He gave me a brown box, tied with a ribbon, etched into the box were the words 'Louis Vuitton.'

I looked up at him. "I can't accept this Carter, it's too much."

He placed his hand on my hands, "Please Freya, it's a gift."

I took my eyes off of him and looked back at the box. I ran my fingers along the edging, I slowly lifted the lid off and there it was: a beautiful black leather neverfull bag.

I placed the box on the floor and threw my arms around his neck. I kissed him softly, "Thank you Carter, but you really didn't have to. Let me pay you back, I can't accept that as a gift." I still had my arms round his neck, it was silent between us.

He put his hands around my waist and pulled him onto

my lap "Call it a bonus," he winked at me.

I frowned, "Please let me pay you back."

He stared at me, "I'll think about it" he smirked.

I shook my head, "Please," I whispered.

He tilted his head back and rested it on the head rest, "I said I would think about it." He leant forward and kissed me on the forehead, "You smell good," he mumbled.

I planted another kiss on his lips, this time I lingered a little longer. "As much as I want to stay kissing you, we are here, and I've got to cook us dinner," he said. I looked out the window and saw this amazing townhouse.

It was like something I had seen in the movies. There were white bollards outside the front with a path that led up to the three steps that led to the black front door. There was a big tree just inside the white wall which sat neatly round the property, on the pavement the trees went for miles. They were all symmetrical and evenly placed. It was so picturesque.

"Welcome to Birchwood" smiling, he lifted me off his lap and exited the car, taking my hand and leading me out onto the pavement, "this is my weekend house, I stay at the apartment during the week." I was speechless, he led me up the stairs and to the front door, "After you Ms. Greene."

CHAPTER TWELVE

I couldn't hide my facial expression when I walked into the grand entrance hall. The floors were a cream marble all the way through, the sweeping staircase to the right off the hall was simply breath-taking. There was a reception room to the left and a living room to the right. I walked slowly down the hallway, I looked back at Carter over my shoulder, I wasn't sure if I was being cheeky for just walking through. He nodded, I smiled as I started walking towards the kitchen. Wow, the kitchen ran along the back of the house. This kitchen was the size of my whole flat, I mean that wasn't hard, but this was amazing.

Carter followed behind me, "Wine?" he asked.

I walked towards him running my hands along the black marble worktops, "Yes please." It was weird seeing him at his home, relaxed.

He poured me a large glass of wine, "Here we go."

I smiled as I took the large glass and took a sip. It was a

crisp white wine, perfectly chilled of course.

"So, what's for dinner? I'm starving."

He looked up from the fridge, "good, steak okay?"

I made myself at home at the breakfast bar, "Steak is perfect – medium rare please chef." I watched as he laughed, his eyes creasing ever so slightly. He looked so beautiful when he laughed. I watched him work his way round the kitchen, "So what is an almost perfect man like you, doing single?" I teased as he turned round from the stove and scoffed.

"Almost perfect?"

I nodded.

"Well, that's what I wanted to talk to you about."

I raised my eyebrows, nearly chocking on my mouthful of wine, oh no, he wasn't going to ask me to be his girlfriend, was he? I've known him just over a week.

I cleared my throat, "Oh did you? What about?"

He threw the tea towel over his shoulder as he served the steak onto the plates, sided with asparagus and dauphinoise potatoes. My belly rumbled, I really was hungry. He sat down next to me and topped my wine up, "Let's eat first," he reasoned. I'm impatient, I didn't want to eat. I wanted to talk.

He looked at his phone and played some music through his sound system. I hadn't noticed but there were speakers in every corner of the room, all of a sudden, the room was filled with a piano and cello. It had become a very relaxed atmosphere. Carter was talking about his mum and that she was coming to stay with him next weekend. I sat and listened to him talk highly of his mother. It was lovely listening how he felt about his family. He was a good cook, the steak melted in my mouth, it was delicious.

He slid off his stool and kissed me on the cheek, "Did you enjoy that?"

Finishing my last mouthful, I nodded, "It was really good, I didn't realise how hungry I was." I stilled in my seat as he leant over me to collect my plate, my breathing fastened.

"What's wrong?" he asked.

I turned in my seat slightly, "You make me nervous." I mumbled.

He looked puzzled "I do?"

I nodded. "I can't read you and that frustrates me. I can't work out what is going on in your head, I'm normally good at gauging people, but you, you don't let on to anything," I furrowed my brow.

He replied, "You don't want to know what is going through my head at the moment." He gave me a sexy half smile, I felt like someone had just let butterflies off in my tummy.

"Come with me, I want to talk to you," he said. I slid off the stool, pulled my t-shirt dress down as subtly as I could, "You don't have to pull that down for my sake, you should be pulling it up." I gasped. "You know you would like that," he teased.

He took my hand and walked me back down the hallway; we turned left into the living room. At the back of the room were some stairs that lead downstairs.

I was silent taking my surroundings in, we walked down the stairs which lead to a large room that was quite easily the same size as the floor above, maybe bigger. There was a skinny long pool, a Jacuzzi in the corner and a seating area. To the left of the seating area was a fully stocked bar.

He led me to the seating area and asked me to sit down. I was nervous, I'm was not ready for a relationship with him, my boss, I hardly know him. Well, I know him a lot better than I did yesterday morning. I blushed thinking back to last night.

"Please don't be nervous," he put both his hands on my knees as he sat opposite me.

"I have a something to ask you..." this was it.

I could feel my palms getting sweaty, I tried to steady my breath.

"Will you be my number seven?" I looked at him confused.

"Your number what?" I shook my head, what was he going on about?

He sat up in his seat and rested his elbows on his knees with his hands together, fingers pointing up to his chin. "Look, let me explain..." he took a deep breath.

I was now intrigued, "I have flavours of the month shall

we say, seven girls who I alternate between, the next two months will be you. I don't see any of the other girls, you don't see anyone else. Once our two months are up, you go back to your day to day life and once your cycle comes around again, I will call you. You will be paid generously in a wage and gifts."

I actually couldn't believe what was coming out of his mouth. I ran my hand through my hair, "Let me see if I understand you properly," I said abruptly.

I stood up and looked down at him, why the bloody hell was he so sexy? It made it hard to be mad at him.

My voice was raised, "You want me, to be a booty call, for a couple of months, until you are bored of me? I'm not some fucking whore Carter, you can't just call me up when you want me and pay me in expensive gifts and cash. Is that what the bag was for? A sweetener, a little taster of what I could be getting?"

He stood up and over me. "No, the bag was a genuine gift, I'm sure I could get you to change your mind," he ran his hands down the side of my body and hitched my t-shirt up slightly, my breath caught.

He moved closer to me, our lips were centimetres apart. He slid his hand higher up my t-shirt and ran his fingers under my knicker line along my bum.

It took everything in me to push his hand away, "I don't think so, call James, I want to go home," I mumbled.

He stepped away from me, "Do you, Freya?"

I swallowed, "Yes."

He reached into his pocket and pulled out his phone "James, please come to Birchwood, Ms. Greene wishes to go home. Yes. No, Now. Thanks," he abruptly put the phone down. He threw it on the small nest of tables next to his seat. I was overlooking the pool, I couldn't do this. This isn't me.

I turned to him, "Can I ask you something?" I could feel the lump in my throat tightening, "the blonde girl in The Ivy..." he looked at me, he looked pissed off, "was she one of your flavours of the month?" I said coldly.

"Yes Freya," he said, annoyed.

I turned back away and looked back at the calm water, "Right." I just nodded. I put my hand up to my face and covered my lips with my thumb. I heard him walking up behind me, he wrapped his arms around me from behind then he nuzzled his head into my shoulder. I watched as his hands crept round the front and rested on my belly, I placed my hands-on top of his, my hands were so small in comparison to his.

I sighed.

He moved, "What's wrong?" he whispered.

I looked over my shoulder at him, "Are you winding me up?"

He turned me round to face him, "Why is this such a problem Freya?"

I pulled away from him, "I'm not a booty call Carter, I actually thought you liked me, but you don't, I'm just a fuck to you."

He grabbed my arm and pulled me into him, "I do like you." He moved my hand down to his groin area, "See." he smirked down at me.

"Don't – I'm not interested Carter. Let's just keep our relationship professional, it's for the best."

He looked away from me and ran his hand through his messy hair, "I don't want to keep our relationship professional. I want our relationship the way it is. Fun."

I tilted my head, "Fun? This isn't fun, this is a booty call, I would be your fuck buddy, friends with benefits – I'm not into that, sorry."

He turned to face me, shit he looks pissed off, "I like to fuck pretty girls, I like to have a selection, so I don't get bored. I like to wine and dine them and show them a good time. You haven't got to worry about having your heartbroken, we both get what we want," I couldn't actually believe what was coming out of his mouth.

"That's not what I want," I corrected him.

He walked over to me, "Is it not?" he hitched my t-shirt up and dropped to his knees.

"Carter, get up," he pushed his hands up my body, pushing my dress higher. He kissed along my knicker line, slowly moving down the centre of my knickers, kissing me a little bit harder once he got to my sweet spot. He ran one of his hands down past my bum, underneath my bum cheek and run his finger underneath me. I moaned softly, the feeling of his fingers caressing me and the silk on my knickers rubbing into me. He slowly flicked his tongue, teasing me. I ran my fingers through his hair and grabbed a handful.

His finger that was running underneath me slowly entered me.

I moaned again which only spurred him on. This was so wrong but so good at the same time.

I wanted to tell him to stop but my body was fixated. His finger was pushing deeper into me, he ran his other hand back down my body and held it at the top of my thigh squeezing it slightly.

He looked up at me and smiled, "You don't want this Freya?"

I couldn't say anything, he had completely intoxicated me. He kept his eyes on me. He removed his finger and slowly started pulling my knickers down and off my feet. He smiled as he looked up at me, "I'm going back to my dessert now."

I felt myself go red, he was so crude. He put his hand back on my thigh and started slowly teasing me with his tongue, he got deeper and faster. I was losing myself, could I be this girl?

I shook my head, "Carter, please, stop. What about James?"

He stopped and looked at me. I could see a glisten on his mouth, "James knows to wait." He stood up and slowly peeled his t-shirt off revealing his toned body. I looked down his body to his 'sex lines' that disappeared into his jeans. He distracted me when he kicked his converse off. He put his arms around me and kissed me, his tongue invading my mouth.

He pulled away looking at me, "Please consider it."

I looked into his beautiful sage eyes, "I can't be this girl – this isn't me."

He let go of me and replied, "It's not like I'm asking you to be my submissive, I'm not a dominant, I just want you to myself, to just fuck and have a good time."

I sighed, "I know you're not, but you are basically asking me to be a prostitute."

He shook his head, "Fine, if that's what you think. Let's go, James is waiting for you."

I found my knickers and put them back on, I watched as Carter put his t-shirt on and slipped his converse on.

I felt cheap, one minute lost in the moment in lust, now I felt like a whore.

We both walked in silence to the main hallway, I picked my bag up that I had left in the entrance hall. Carter opened the door and walked me out to James. As usual James gave me a lovely smile, he knew. He knows what this arrangement was.

Tonight was the first time I actually looked at James. He had short cropped blonde hair, piercing blue eyes with a peachy complexion.

He opened the passenger door for me, "Evening Freya" he said as I got into the car.

Carter stood on the pavement with his hands in his pockets, his eyes were burning into mine, we just stared at each other. "Bye Carter," I swallowed, the lump slowly creeping back into my throat.

James shut the door as I sat back in the chair and breathed, I could feel the tears starting to prick in my eyes - I couldn't stop them.

I looked at the Louis Vuitton box on the floor, I kicked it back under the seat, I didn't want his gift. Just as James started to drive off, my passenger door swung open.

Carter jumped in and looked at me, "Baby, why are you crying, please don't cry!" he said in a low soft voice, his Australian twang coming through.

He put his arm round me and pulled me into him, I laid into him, not moving, neither of us saying a word. I just wanted to go home, and for the first time in a long while, I meant Elsworth.

CHAPTER THIRTEEN

We pulled up outside my apartment. Neither of us had spoken for the duration of the journey. James pulled up to the kerb and opened my door, I leant off of Carter and left the car.

I nodded at James and he gave me a weak smile, he must have felt so awkward. I started walking towards my apartment stairs when I felt him behind me. "Freya, please. Don't leave it like this."

I turned to face him, tears filling my eyes again. "I can't do it," I stumbled over my words.

He took my hand as we stood looking at each other.

"Let me go, please." I looked at the floor, with that he reluctantly let go.

"Bye," I mumbled as I walked into my apartment block. As I walked up the stairs to my front door I looked back and saw Carter still standing outside the communal door.

I let myself in to my house and locked the door behind

me, then walked into my bedroom and threw myself on my bed. I just wanted to go to sleep and forget out the last couple of hours.

When I woke up I so felt disorientated. I looked at the time: 2:30am, I groaned. I got up, I had to get out of these clothes. I walked into the shower and let the hot water wash everything away, my stomach was in knots.

I stepped out of the shower and walked into my bedroom, I grabbed a top and pyjama bottoms and crawled back into bed. I looked at my phone, missed calls from Carter. Why was he calling me? I have nothing to say to him. I had a message from Laura asking how my evening had been and that it was nice seeing me earlier; I text her back telling her I would speak to her tomorrow. I lay in bed with my mind racing, why was this bothering me so much? I didn't realise how much I liked him, why couldn't I have felt like this with Ethan, why did I have to settle for this idiot. I rolled my eyes, oh god, and work, now it's going to be awkward. I made sure my phone was on silent and rolled over, I needed to sleep.

After the worst night's sleep I'd had in ages, I decided to get out of bed - it was 7am. I felt like I had grit in my eyes. I made my way into the kitchen and put the kettle on. Tilly jumped on the worktop and nuzzled my arm, I smiled and gave her a scratch behind her ear, she thanked me with a purr. She obviously knew I needed some comforting. I picked her up and stood staring out the window for a few minutes, I just couldn't stop thinking about him, my heart hurt. I felt like I had been kicked in my stomach, I don't remember even feeling like this with Jake.

I was bought back down to earth by getting scalded by the steam from the kettle, "Ouch, fuck it!" I dropped the cat and ran to the sink to run my arm under it.

After the sting had gone, I re-boiled the kettle and poured myself a cup of tea. I sat on the sofa resting my cup on my knees. I turned the TV on just to have some background noise. I heard my phone vibrate so I dragged myself off of the sofa and picked it up off of the worktop. It was Ethan:

Hey, still ok for that coffee today? Let me know, Ethan

Oh god, I forgot I arranged a coffee with Ethan. Well I had arranged coffee before he turned up and kissed me. I typed a reply agreeing to meet him at 10 in the Starbucks on the corner. I can't avoid him, plus he makes me laugh and I need that at the moment.

I'm looking forward to coming back and having an early night ready for work in the morning, I need to just get on with my work and keep a professional relationship with Carter.

I put a bit of make up on then put my skinny jeans on and a baggy t-shirt and my flip flops. I grabbed my bits and shut the door. I started walking down the stairs and there at the bottom was Carter. My heart stopped. "Freya…" he said calmly. It took everything in me to walk past him, "I can't stop thinking about you" he sighed.

I looked back at him, "Carter, I've told you I can't do this, I'm not that woman. Please, can we just be amicable for work and just leave it at that?"

His eyes didn't leave mine. He even looks hot when his mad, I wanted to kiss him, tell him to just want me and only me. "That's what you want," he asked.

No, I don't want that, but you don't just want me, I said in my head.

"Is it?" he asked again.

I looked at him and he looked tired, his eyes dark, his skin pale. I sighed and took a step towards him, I lifted my hand to his face and rested it on his cheek, "No, I don't want this. Carter you make me feel things I didn't even know I could feel."

I slowly took my hand away and knotted my fingers, "I don't want to be like that, like what you asked, it's not something I can be, to share you and only be used when you want to use me."

I heard him breathe in deeply, "I don't want to share you, like you don't really want to share me" I whispered.

He just stayed silent, "So that's why it isn't going to work."

I shrugged and took a step back and before I could bite my tongue it came out, "It's like a fucked up version of Snow White and the seven dwarfs, except it would be Mr Cole and the seven whores!" I snarled.

He smirked at me, "And what's wrong with that?" he murmured.

I rolled my eyes at him: let's see how this sits with him I thought "There is nothing wrong with that if that's what you want to do, I don't want to do that. Anyway I've got to run, I'm meeting Ethan," I said with a smile.

His smirk had gone, his eyes glazed over, I could see his body tense up at his name.

"I will speak to you tomorrow at work no doubt, have a nice afternoon." And with that, I walked out, my heart was thumping through my chest, my throat felt tight where I was panicking, my palms were sweaty. I daren't look back. I walked as quickly as I could to Starbucks.

I walked into Starbucks, I couldn't see Ethan straightaway. Just as I was about to give up a lady moved slightly. There he was: curly blonde hair, deep hazel eyes and his smile. He stood up and rested his hand on my hip and kissed my cheek, "Hey, I'm sorry about last night, I really am."

I smiled at him, "It's fine, honestly." He handed me a white Americano, it was so needed. I sat down opposite him and took a sip of my coffee, it hit the right spot.

"So, how's Mr Suit?" he run his hand round the back of his neck. I reached out and put my hands on the table.

"Mr Suit is pretty pissed off right about now," I said with a smirk. He met my hands in the middle of the table, and gently touched them. It made me feel uneasy, especially with how I've just left things with Carter.

I slowly moved my hand away and bit my lip. We didn't have to say anything, Ethan knew exactly what was going on in my head; he just nodded at me.

We sat and chatted about our week ahead, Laura and Tyler's wedding and a date that Ethan was going on Tuesday evening. A pang of disappoint hit me, but what could I really be disappointed about? I chose Carter over him, I didn't give him a chance, us a chance.

It made me think of how Ethan and I would get on, he reminds me of a typical surfer boy - cool, good looking and beautiful curly hair. I could see him with a surf board. I shook the thoughts from my head. I say I chose Carter, I didn't. I gave him up because I didn't want to be one of his girls. I just wanted him for myself, was that too much to ask.

"Freya, you okay?"

I looked at him, "Sorry, I didn't sleep very well last night, just thinking of the events that unfolded last night."

He looked concerned.

"It's fine, just Mr Suit issues, but I don't want to bore you with them."

He nodded at me then said, "Just remember I'm always here if you need me, as a friend, and maybe, just maybe you will let me take you on a date, you know, because I was such an arse?"

I sat and thought for a while, "I'll think about it," and

smiled at him, "I've really got to get going, I've got to sort some bits for work. Let me know a date that's good for you and we will go have our 'date'" I teased. I gave him a hug goodbye, he held on a little longer, "Thank you for my coffee," I smiled and said goodbye.

I took a slow walk home. I pulled my phone out of my bag – eight missed calls, all from Carter.

I'm not calling him, let him stew. I took a walk through the park - I watched the children playing, the couples in love eating picnics and frolicking, the families enjoying their long Sunday walks. I left the park and walked down the pavements up to my apartments, I looked up at the trees that ran down the street, black iron fencing round each trunk. You forget how pretty your city is when you live in it every day.

I walked up the communal stairs and stopped at my letterbox, nothing important, Domino's pizza leaflet was the only thing I was interested in.

I walked up the stairs in the communal hallway to my front door and stopped in my path. There, sitting outside my front door was Carter, his face looked strained, his lips pursed and tight, "Well look who has returned from her date." he hissed.

"It wasn't a date, I met my friend for a coffee." He shook his head.

"You met 'him' from downstairs!" he raised his voice, emphasizing the 'him.'

I held onto the bannisters, "Firstly, him from

downstairs has a name. It's Ethan."

He slowly stood from the floor and walked over to me, "I have been sitting here for three hours waiting for you, waiting for you to come home from being with him." I tightened my grip, he stood looking over me, "I don't want to share you," he said holding my chin and tilting my head back.

I closed my eyes as he hovered his lips over mine, I whispered, "I don't want to share you, but it doesn't work that way does it?"

I opened my eyes and looked up at him, he didn't say anything - he looked like a lost boy. I slowly ran my fingers through his hair then slowly down the back of his head, grabbing a little bit of his hair at the nape of his neck. I pulled him towards me and kissed him, our lips slowly moving in sync with each other.

Even though I was only kissing him last night it felt like it had been a lifetime. His kiss began to get fiercer, his tongue caressing mine on every movement.

I ran my hands slowly down his back and felt his muscles begin to relax. His hands rested on my hips then moved down to my bum.

I pulled away and took his hand, walking him up to my front door, his hands slowly moving round my waist as I opened the door. I turned around to look at him, his hands back on my waist, he lifted me gently and carried me through the front door and straight through to my bedroom.

He stood me down and slowly removed my t-shirt over

my head then he pulled my hair out of my messy bun and let it fall down around my breasts. His hands were on my body, he planted kisses on my neck, tracing them slowly up to my chin line and slowly round to my lips, I took a deep breath, "Carter..." I murmured.

He replied with a deep, "Mmm..."

I looked at him, "What are we doing? You've made it clear what you want."

He bit his lip. "I want you Freya, you want me why has this got to be so hard?"

I sighed, "You are the one making it hard, you are being greedy, I'm not enough for you. The fact that you have six girls you alternate between, and then you want to make me a seventh..."

He bowed his head and slowly removed his hands from my body.

"Exactly, I'm not enough, you can't even deny it."

He slid his jumper up his arm and looked at his watch, "I've got to go, I've got stuff to sort out," he muttered.

I stood there, mouth open, "You are just going to go without saying anything?" I shook my head, "Fine, go," I said bluntly.

He kissed me on the forehead and walked out of my bedroom. I didn't move, just stood there playing over the last few minutes over and over again.

I heard my front door shut then I walked out of the bedroom and just looked at my door. He has actually just gone, no explanation, just left. I was confused, upset and angry. I picked up the vase I had put his white roses he sent me last week and threw it at my door as I screamed. The vase shattered into a million pieces, the roses falling to the floor. The water splashed up the walls and door and pooled on the floor. Why did I have to fall for him? Haven't I been through enough with Jake and now Carter?

I slid down my hallway wall and bought my knees up to my chest, wrapping my arms around them and sinking my head to meet them. The tears started flowing - *I can't do this, I can't keep tormenting myself.*

I unlocked my phone and put Spotify on. I needed some noise; my apartment was way too quiet. A song came on by Nina Nesbitt called Somebody Special, I sat and listened to the words and scoffed, this was exactly how I felt.

I rolled my eyes and said to myself *'why can't you tear yourself away from your fucked-up arrangement'.* I skipped the song and rested my head back on the wall.

As I sat there listening to my playlist, all of a sudden, I heard a knock on the door which made me jump from my thoughts. "Go away!" I shouted.

"It's me, open the door!" a voice that sounded like Laura's shouted back. What was she doing here? I pulled myself up off the floor and stepped round the flowers and broken glass.

I opened the door, "What the hell is going on Freya? Look at you! Your eyes are bloodshot and smudged, you look like shit!" she looked at the floor, "and why is this on the floor?" she was eyeing up the broken vase.

I looked at the floor.

"Let me in so we can sort this mess out. I've been worried about you, I haven't heard from you since Saturday afternoon," she said, her face full of concern.

I threw myself at her and hugged her as I felt myself getting upset again.

"Come on, let me put the kettle on," she said through a smile "and you can explain everything."

CHAPTER FOURTEEN

Laura walked over to me in my cosy living room. Passing me a hot cup of tea, she sat down next to me. She was an angel. She told me to go and sit on the sofa while she cleared up the broken glass and mopped the water up, she also put the flowers in the bin, "So, do you want to fill me in?"

I looked at her while taking a sip of my tea - she did make a good cuppa. Laura's motto is 'tea makes everything better.' She was right; tea is definitely always the answer. Or wine. Wine definitely makes things better.

I sighed "Ugh, it's just stuff with Carter, it shouldn't be this complicated this early on..."

She clocked her head, "So, are you two official then?"

I shook my head, "Not quite," I mumbled.

"Sorry Freya, I'm confused, what is actually going on between you two? You slept together, is that all that's happened?" she asked.

"I wish," I said under my breath.

"Right well can you tell me what's going on then? It can't be good looking at the state you are in at the moment," she said.

I took a deep breath and started telling her what had been happening. It felt good to talk to someone about it rather than just dealing with Carter then having to cope with it by myself. She was pretty upset with what I said, and she told me I deserved better than him.

"I know I do, but I feel something for him that I can't explain. I feel like he brings me to life, like I have been waiting for him..."

She rolled her eyes at me. "Freya, he's trying to make you do something you don't want to do. How can you think he cares about you if his making such a deal out of it?" She was right, I couldn't argue with her. I gently reminded her that I hadn't agreed to be what he wanted and that was why he left like he did.

She put her arm around me and gave me a little squeeze. "Anyway, enough about my dramas, what's been going on in the life of Laura and Tyler?" asked with a smile.

"Well before we get into that, can you go put your t-shirt on?" I looked down. Oh god, I had been in such a state that I hadn't even put my t-shirt back on!

"One sec," I ran off the sofa and returned with my t-shirt, "sorry." I smiled.

She shook her head, "I'm not even going to ask."

After a couple of hours talking about all stuff wedding,

Laura had to go, "I've got bits to sort for work tomorrow. You should hopefully be able to carry on writing your blog piece for the site now? It was only a week's break wasn't it?"

I had completely forgotten about that, "I don't think I'm in the right place at the moment, so if Jools does offer it back to me I will kindly decline. I don't think You Magazine is quite ready for my 'and the seven whores' piece," I laughed. She gave me a kiss on the cheek and told me she would see me tomorrow and if I needed anything to call her.

Monday morning was soon upon us, I didn't really want to go into work and face Jools or Carter.

I looked at the time, 6:05am, sod it. I opened my messages and typed Jools name in the search bar. I typed a quick message stating I had a sickness bug and would be in on Wednesday/Thursday and that if anything was needed I was happy to do some work from home.

I didn't even care at that moment if she told me not to come back. I put my phone back on the bedside table, got myself comfortable and went back to sleep. *Why do I always fall for idiots?* I thought as I drifted off.

I woke about 9am. I felt a lot better having gone back to sleep for a couple of hours, but it still didn't stop this pain in my chest. I honestly felt like someone had ripped my heart out of my chest.

I finally pulled myself out of bed and walked to the kitchen, Tilly had obviously gone over to Erin's house; she was clearly fed up of me moping about. I bet Carter wasn't feeling like this, he was probably with one his 'ladies' forgetting all about me. I frowned at the thought.

I put the kettle on and made myself a cup of tea. While sipping it I started thinking about Ethan and how things were left, I thought that maybe I should send him a message. Before I could stop my stupid thoughts, we had somehow arranged to meet for lunch this afternoon. This definitely was not a good idea.

After having a quick shower, I walked into my bedroom and decided what to wear as it was an overcast day but warm. I decided on a pair of washed out dungarees with a white t-shirt underneath and my white converse.

I pulled my hair up into a messy bun and applied just enough make up for my eye bags. I sighed at myself in the mirror. I was looking forward to seeing Ethan but just wish I would have stopped myself texting him so eagerly.

I heard a knock at the door. I grabbed my bits and opened it - there he was with a boyish smile on his face, his blonde curly hair, his brown eyes gleaming and his imperfect crooked smile.

"Hey," he smiled at me.

"Hey," I smiled back at him. I walked slowly out of the flat, feeling anxious. I felt like Carter would be standing at the bottom of the stairs waiting to catch me as if I was going behind his back. It was unnerving and I didn't like it.

"What's wrong?" Ethan could sense my worry.

I locked the flat door and started walking down the

stairs, "Nothing, it just feels a bit weird."

He nodded, "Don't worry about it, let's go."

I put my sunglasses on and walked out onto the street. A taxi was already waiting outside for us. I jumped in and Ethan followed.

"Relax, Freya, I'm not going to jump on you," he laughed, "We are friends aren't we?"

I let out a sigh. It just felt weird seeing as we went on a couple of dates and now things were over between Carter and I, I didn't want him to think I was giving him the green light. "I know we are, just feels a bit weird don't you think?"

He shook his head, "No, I don't."

It was only a short taxi ride before we were at the restaurant, Ethan had picked a small Italian about ten minutes from the flat. I had never been there before but had heard it was lovely. Ethan refused to take any cash off me for the taxi so I said I would buy him lunch, although, I had a feeling he would refuse that as well.

We were greeted by a young Italian woman who showed us to our seat at the back of the restaurant. I put my sunglasses in my bag and checked my phone, secretly hoping I would have a message from Carter. The disappointment hit me when I had nothing except my weekly text from Domino's telling me about their deals of the week. I silenced my phone and put it back in my bag.

The pretty waitress stood patiently at our table whilst we decided on our drinks. I quickly grabbed the wine menu and started scanning the white wines to see if anything on there took my fancy.

"I will have a Peroni please," Ethan flashed her his charming smile and she blushed slightly. She broke her gaze and then asked me what I would like.

"Erm, can I have a bottle of the Sancerre please?" I smiled, I could feel Ethan staring at me. "Don't judge me," I scowled at him and he held his hands up to say sorry. He then looked back at the waitress and she gave him an awkward smile and shrug, she quickly took our drink menus and laid two dinner menus in front of us.

"Is there a problem?" I asked him.

"No, not at all, just it's 12pm on a Monday and you've ordered a bottle of wine to yourself," he muttered.

"And your point is?" I questioned him, "I'm 29 Ethan, if I want to have a bottle of wine to myself I will, I've had a really shitty weekend so a bottle of wine isn't going to hurt anyone!" I snapped.

The waitress must have felt the tension as she opened my bottle of wine and just started pouring, looking at me to tell her when was enough. I literally left it till last minute when my glass was brimming, "Perfect," I smiled at her.

Again, Ethan and the waitress gave each other a knowing look. She obviously thought we were on a date and that it was going horribly wrong so, I decided to tell her what was actually going on. "Just in case you were wondering," I cleared my throat, "this isn't a date, we are friends. I have just been dumped, well not just, last night, but still pretty recent. This isn't an awkward first date where the poor man has ended up with a crazy lady!" I took a big sip of my wine, "So if you are interested in him, Ethan, then take his number. He is a wonderful guy and has good taste in home furnishings."

She just stared at me with her mouth open, I looked over at Ethan and he had his head in his hands shaking it side to side, "I actually think you two would make a lovely couple," I added.

After about five minutes of Ethan apologising to the young waitress, I had already sank half the bottle of wine, and we were still waiting for our food. I heard footsteps behind me as Ethan approached our table to sit back down. "What the hell is a matter with you!?" he asked sternly.

"Nothing is a matter with me, I ordered a drink, I was judged, she then assumed that poor Ethan was on a terrible date with a crazy lady so I thought I would settle it. Plus, like I said, I think you two would make a nice couple," I smiled at him, "so if it does work out then you have me too thank!" I laughed.

"Freya, I know you are upset about Carter, but don't be like this. This isn't you. I'm not saying don't drink, but slow down," he looked at me, "don't let that idiot make you like this, you are so much better than this and you know it."

I slowly put my glass down and pushed it away, he did have a point. "Fine," I sighed, "I won't guzzle it down, but to be honest, you are lucky I didn't order twenty vodka shots." I rolled my eyes at him, "I'm just struggling with it all, it all happened so quickly between me and Carter, and it ended just as fast."

I put my head in my hands. "This is what happens when you dive headfirst into something with someone you actually don't know a lot about."

I felt his hands gently pull mine away from my face, "Don't blame yourself for this babe, this isn't your fault. He is an absolute cock womble for giving up on you this easy. You are such an amazing, beautiful, funny woman. You deserve so much more," he gave me a slight smile and I couldn't help but smile back.

"Anyway, I totally gave her my number, going out with her Friday. She is hot, and definitely my type," he sat back in his chair grinning like a Cheshire cat.

After a much quieter dinner than it started, Ethan and I were walking back up to my flat.

"So, you back at work tomorrow sick note?" he laughed.

"Maybe, see how I feel tomorrow, probably go back in on Wednesday. Breaks my week up a bit, plus it gives me a couple of days Carter free, so if I do see him or hear from him, I should hopefully have a clear head."

Ethan nodded, "That makes sense," he smiled, "anyway, I will let you go."

I smiled at him, "Thank you for lunch, you really didn't have to pay for me, I wanted to pay for it." I turned to unlock my door, dropping my bag just inside while I said bye to

Ethan.

He stepped towards me, "Let's not leave it till you break up with someone next time, ay?" he said grinning. I really did love his crooked smile.

"I promise, we will go for lunch dates and coffee dates more often," I smiled and stepped backwards into the flat. Ethan stepped closer and before I could register what was happening, he kissed me, not just a little kiss on the cheek but a deep, slow kiss.

I pulled away, "Ethan, what are you doing?"

He looked down at the floor. "Sorry Freya, I just, I just needed to-" I stepped away from him and walked into the flat, shutting the door. I could feel him still standing on the other side.

I slumped myself down on the sofa trying to digest what had happened, we were friends, he was seeing other people, we never made ourselves exclusive and he never actually said he liked me like that.

I heard my phone beep, my heart raced hoping it was Carter but of course it wasn't, it was Ethan, apologising again. He was trying to explain that he just wanted to see if he felt anything more for me than 'just friends.' I rolled my eyes and threw my phone on the other side of the sofa. It was just one thing after another.

CHAPTER FIFTEEN

Thursday morning soon came around. I went into the bathroom to get ready. I decided on a fitted faux leather pencil skirt, buttoned white shirt with ruffled sleeves and a small ruffle round the collar. I tucked my shirt in and slipped into my Louboutin's. I roughly ran the straighteners over my hair and checked my makeup. My bags were covered, that was all I cared about.

Once I stepped off the train I stopped at the Starbucks near work and grabbed myself a grande macchiato. I needed something a little stronger than a latte. I also picked Jools up an Americano like I did most mornings, even though she tells me she doesn't like them, which I struggle with seeing as in my interview that was part of the job role.

I walked through the glass doors of the reception. "Morning Sid, morning Rachel." They both wished me good morning as I headed to the lift. I walked into my office, put my coffee down on my desk and walked into Jools's office.

"Good morning Jools," I dropped her coffee as I entered her office. There in front of me in deep conversation with Jools, was Carter.

They both looked in my direction as they heard the coffee cup hit the tiles, "Oh, I'm so sorry Jools!" I could feel Carter's eyes on me all the time as I bent down as gracefully as I could.

It certainly wasn't easy in a leather pencil skirt. I picked the coffee cup up, "I'll go get some tissue," I whispered. Jools just nodded at me, Carter had a smirk on his face.

I'm glad this amused him. I walked into the kitchen area and grabbed as much blue roll as I could, my heart was thumping. What the bloody hell was he doing here? Oh god, maybe he was taking me off his work load? I suppose that would be a blessing in disguise, but that would also mean he didn't want to work with me anymore, which would also mean I would have no reason to see him or contact him anymore...

I ran back into Jools's office and bent down to clear the mess up. I went to stand and lost my balance and fell forward on all fours, 'why Freya, why?' I thought.

I looked up at them both as I felt the crimson spreading across my face. Before I could move, Carter bent down in front of me, whispering so that only I could hear, "You really should wear more suitable clothing, that skirt is a bit tight, maybe I could help you out of it later on after dinner?"

I gave him evils, he took my arm and gently helped me

up. I brushed myself down and straightened my shirt, "Sorry again, I will go and make you a fresh coffee."

Jools stood up out of her chair, "That won't be necessary Freya," I swallowed, this was it, I was going to lose my job.

I knotted my fingers as I waited to hear what she had to say, "From today you will no longer be working for You Magazine."

My face dropped, my eyes darted from her to Carter, "What? No Jools, please don't do this, I love my job, I don't want to go!"

She looked at Carter and frowned, "Freya, who said anything about you having to leave?"

I threw her a puzzled look.

"Mr Cole wants you moved over to Cole Enterprise. He has been very happy with your work and wants you to start immediately!"

I looked at Carter, what was he thinking? "Oh," was all I could say, "I've only been doing the job for a couple of weeks." I felt my eyes darting back and forth between them.

"Well you've obviously been doing something right Freya for him to feel this way."

He smirked at that. "No pun intended, Ms. Greene," he said after clearing his throat.

I just nodded, "Okay, so am I finishing my day here? I've got work to finish."

Jools just shook her head, "No, you are going to leave with Mr Cole shortly. I have a temp replacement coming in till I find a suitable match."

I nodded again, "Okay, well thank you for all you've done for me Jools, I honestly cannot thank you enough!" I smiled at her. "Mr Cole, thank you for this opportunity, I hope I don't let you down." Before I could hear his response, I walked out the office and sat at my desk.

What the hell was happening? I put my head in my hands and groaned.

After five minutes, I heard him walking out of Jools's office, "Ready, Freya?" he smiled at me.

I pushed back off my chair and grabbed my bag then I walked away from my desk and towards the big glass doors that lead to the communal hallway.

Before stepping out, I looked over my shoulder at Jools and smiled, she returned a smile and held her hand up. I walked out and stood waiting for the lift when I felt Carter's hand rest on the small of my back, "You look lovely today," he whispered in my ear. I didn't say anything - I just stood there in silence until the lift doors opened.

As the lift halted at the ground floor I walked over to Rachel and hugged her. I promised to keep in touch and that we would meet for lunch. She looked as confused as I felt. I then said bye to Sid and walked outside onto the busy street.

James was there waiting with the door open, "Morning Freya." I smiled at him and got into the car, shortly followed by Carter. James shut the door and walked round to the front of the car, "What the hell do you think you are doing?!" I shouted, "Who do you think you are taking me from my job? I loved my job and now, well I don't even know what I'm going to be doing now!" I felt my phone vibrate, I bet it was Laura asking me what was going on.

"Calm down Freya, I want you to work for me, so that's exactly what you are doing!"

I stared at him.

"I own You Magazine, so if I want to take an employee that I think will benefit my company, I will," he said with a grin.

I sat back in the chair and took a deep breath, "That's not fair, I was happy in my job, I knew my job. Now, now I don't even know what I will be doing, where I will be working..."

He put his hand on my knee, "Baby, please don't stress about that. We are not going to work today, we are going to my place. There's a few things I need to speak to you about before you start at Cole Enterprise tomorrow."

I looked out the window, "Fine," I mumbled.

I took my phone out my bag and looked - yup, as I had guessed, it was Laura. Carter was on his phone replying to emails, so I typed a response to her

Don't. I feel like I've been kidnapped, don't even know where my new office is. Going back to Carter's apartment to "talk work"

Will call you later, love you xx

I threw my phone in my bag and dropped it on the floor. Carter looked up from his phone. I put my finger up to my mouth, as if silencing a small child. I didn't want to talk to him.

After fifteen minutes of silence, we pulled up outside a beautiful building. I looked up at it out of the window, there were big windows going the whole way along the front walls. There was a concierge standing outside the revolving doors, and from what I could see, marble floors running through the building.

Carter was already out of the car and he had opened the door for me instead of James, he just sat quietly in the front. I took his hand and said thank you as we walked up to the building. "Welcome back Mr Cole," the doorman said in a cheery tone. Carter just nodded at him. I followed him through the long hallway to the lifts, the building was beautiful. Even though it had a modern feel it still had all of its old characteristics. The lift doors opened, and Carter held his hand out, I smiled and walked into the lift with him following behind me.

I didn't know what this was about, I was anxious. I was fidgeting with my shirt when he looked at me, "Don't be nervous," he said in a calm voice "you have nothing to worry about." I dropped my hands and held onto my bag handles, at least that way it gave my hands something to do.

As the lift doors opened, I slowly stepped out into the

apartment. I dropped my bag to the floor. The first thing I noticed was the views over the city, they were truly breath taking.

As I walked towards the windows, the living room sat to the right. There were big patio doors leading to a small terrace area, walking back through from the living room was a dining room. The ceilings were high, the room was light with an eight-seater white marble dining table and high back grey material chairs.

I slowly walked down the hallway off of the dining room and into an open planned kitchen. There was a breakfast bar, this time in white marble with flecks of gold embedded into it. This place was completely different from his townhouse.

It was a large space with a smaller table in the corner overlooking the views and a corner sofa with a coffee table over the other side of the kitchen. The downstairs of this apartment was modern, not like the townhouse, the townhouse had a homelier feel to it.

I walked towards the staircase which was off of the dining room. As I slowly walked up the stairs, I couldn't help but feel at home - it was breath-taking.

I turned right and walked down the long narrow hallway which lead to the master bedroom. I walked slowly through noticing the walk-in dresser room to my right. I made my way into dressing room, it was a similar size to my apartment, it was ridiculous, honestly who needed a dressing room this big? I looked to the left and noticed a very modern black and gold marble bathroom, the focus piece in this room was the bath, there were two steps taking you up to the bath which was big enough for about five people. On the bath were big ornate gold taps and a shower head, to the side was a shower with a single pane of glass as a shower curtain and a flat level floor so no need for a tray.

I felt like I was in heaven. Carter came up behind me, "So, what do you think?"

I turned around to face him, "It's beautiful," even the bathroom had big picture windows overlooking the city. That was my favourite part.

Before he finished giving me the tour of the penthouse, he showed me where the utility room was, then he showed me two more bedrooms both with ensuites, a main bathroom, a library, an office, a bar and wine cellar plus a small apartment upstairs big enough and fully equipped for his house keepers to live in. *Who actually has housekeepers?!* I thought to myself.

We came back downstairs and walked into the living room. I slipped my shoes off and sat looking out the window as Carter came and sat next to me, "I brought you here to talk Freya."

I turned to face him, "About what?" I asked inquisitively.

"I want to try, I want to try and just be with you," he said quietly. I shook my head. "Freya, please. After I left your apartment yesterday I couldn't stop thinking about you, I don't want to lose you, I had a taste of that yesterday when my actions pushed you towards Ethan. I can't get you out of my head, I haven't slept, I've hardly eaten. So, when I left I called my girls over, I sat down and told them that I needed a break, I needed to work through some things, something I feel very strongly about..."

I didn't say anything, just listened to him as he spoke, he cleared his throat, "So, I said I would put them on six months full pay until I know how this is going, this being me and you."

He looked at me, waiting for me to say something. I took a deep breath and put my hands on his knee, "Carter, I can't let you do that. You have needs, you like to switch it up and not be stuck with the same girl. I get that -"

He moved closer to me, interrupting me "Freya, I just want you," he whispered.

CHAPTER SIXTEEN

"Say something, please," he said.

The truth was, I didn't know what to say. I was happy, angry, overwhelmed, nervous and scared all at the same time, "You've really done that for me?" I mumbled as I looked at my hands.

He took my left hand and nodded, "I really have."

I looked at him, his eyes were glistening from the warm sun shining through the windows, his skin glowing. "Okay."

His eyes lit up, "Okay!? Really?"

I smiled and said, "Let's just take this one step at a time, we've known each other a couple of weeks, there is still a lot we don't know about each other."

He nodded in agreement, "One step at a time," he smiled.

I shuffled back on the sofa, "I would like to know what this new role is that you have for me."

He stood up and took his suit jacket off, "I've got a few

new companies Cole Enterprises are looking to buy, I would like you to be my Virtual Assistant." He could see the 'are you serious?' look on my face and he laughed in response, "Hear me out, please - a virtual assistant is a remote freelancer who helps small companies and consultants with some of the more routine tasks, like writing letters, blogs, columns, press releases and even proof reading. Now, I know you enjoyed the manuscripts so this would still be in your job description. Most of these companies we buy are in a bad financial state, so there is normally a lot of work to be done, most of that writing. It's a temporary position, just until they are up and running. You will then have the choice to move into one of our existing companies and enroll in any job."

He could see I was unsure, "Please, it's just a fill gap." I nodded, at least I could move to another company once this was complete, hopefully over to CPH.

"Now can we move onto more pressing matters?"

I looked at him, "What would that be then?" slowly getting up from the sofa and walking backwards away from him.

He sat still, his eyes not leaving mine. "Like getting you out of that skirt, I've been wanting to do it since you stepped into Jools's office this morning..." he slowly stood up and walked over to me, I stood with my back against the breakfast bar, my heart beat getting faster as he moved closer towards me.

He clasped my face in his hands and kissed me, his

hands slowly moving down to my waist as his fingers found my zip on the back of my skirt. He pulled his lips away from mine as he slowly undid my zip and gently tugged my skirt, so it fell to the floor.

I stepped out of it, his eyes marveling over my body. He moved to my shirt buttons, undoing them slowly while planting soft kisses on my neck, he slid my shirt down my arms and watched it fall.

He stepped back and looked me up and down, "I like this underwear, this is what you wore on our date." He moved my hair behind my shoulders, I reached up to him and undid his shirt buttons, as I was undoing them I started kissing his chest slowly, following my hands down.

I dropped to my knees, looking up at him. He shrugged his shirt off as I started to undo his belt. I unbuttoned his suit trousers and slowly slid them down his legs. He really was a god, he was toned in all the right places, his trimmed snail trail enticing me to his boxers.

I ran my finger along the hem then followed my fingers with kisses, his fingers gently playing with my hair. I bit my lip as I slowly slid his boxers down. I smiled as his thick shaft sprung from them.

I took him into my hands and slowly started moving them up and down. I could see his arousal starting to show. I stopped my hands at the base of his cock and took him into my mouth, he tasted sweet.

He took a deep breath and tightened his grip round my

hair, "Oh, Freya," he moaned, I carried on slowly teasing him with my tongue and then taking him back into my mouth. I continued this rhythm until he was ready to climax, "Ah," he whispered as he hit his orgasm.

After he had finished I looked up at him, "Did you enjoy that?" I said in a silky voice. As I stood up he pushed me against the breakfast bar, finding my mouth and kissing me, I could still taste him. His kiss grew deeper as his tongue caressed mine.

He lifted me up onto the breakfast bar and spread my legs apart. He run his hand up my back and took a small handful of my hair, he gently pulled my head back.

"I can't wait to fuck you, I am going to drive you wild," he whispered in my ear. A shiver ran down my spine, the dull ache deep in my stomach started.

He let go of my hair and slowly undid my bra then he took both of my breasts into his hands as he slowly flicked his tongue over my nipples, then taking my breast into his mouth and sucking. He dropped to his knees and moved my knickers aside, his finger slipped into me while his thumb was stroking my sweet spot. I moaned as he continued to slowly move his finger in and out of me, his thumb matching his slow rhythm. His left hand gently cupped my breast.

He looked up at me through his long eyelashes and smirked. He stopped with his thumb and replaced the motion with his tongue. I looked down at him and watched as he moved slowly over my sex, his tongue flicking and caressing me, his finger still slowly massaging me inside.

I could feel my orgasm starting to build, "Carter, stop," I whispered, he slowly pulled his finger out and stood up, my arousal on his lips.

He took me round the hips and slid me forward, he stood over me and slowly entered me, I moaned as he started to move. My legs were wrapped around his body, my hands gripping onto the edge of the breakfast bar, our lips meeting.

We were lost in each other, his sweet slow moves making my orgasm climb higher and higher inside my body. Just as I was getting to my peak he stopped. He picked me up and carried me to his bedroom.

He put me down at the foot of the bed. I was so hungry for him. I pushed him down onto the bed and crawled towards him, I straddled myself over him, slowly taking all of him in. A gasp left my body as he began to fill me, he felt so good. I started to move slowly, watching him the whole time.

His hands rested gently on my hips as I was thrusting them back and forth. He sat up and cradled me, taking my breast into his mouth and started to slowly caress my nipple with his tongue. I mirrored his rhythm with my hips, there it was, the sweet feel of my orgasm building again, "Carter," I whispered, "keep going, please." He stared slowly thrusting his hips up to meet my movements, his tongue still flicking and caressing my nipple, the sensation of him inside me, his fingers and mouth around my breasts tipped me over the edge, "I'm going to come..." as soon as the words left my lips

I let go around him as he followed.

"Am I okay to have shower?" I asked as he looked up from his phone.

"Freya, you don't need to ask."

I rolled my eyes, "It's called manners."

I walked through the dressing room and into the bathroom and stepped into the shower, letting the water run over me. I felt him stand behind me, his hands wrapped around my waist as he gently kissed my neck.

After the shower Carter said he was going to his office to tie up some loose ends, so I headed to the kitchen. I opened the fridge and found some bits to make a stir fry, I decided to cook us both a bit of lunch as I was starving.

After finding my way around the kitchen I walked up to his office to let him know lunch was done but he was on the phone when I got to the door so I mouthed that lunch was ready. I walked back down the hallway and sat at the breakfast bar waiting for him to join me.

After about ten minutes he walked into the kitchen, "You should have started without me baby," he kissed me on the forehead then he walked over to the fridge and took a bottle of white wine out and took two glasses from the cupboard. Next, he poured us both a glass. He held up his glass in a toasting gesture, "To new business adventures, and personal, obviously!" he smirked, we met glasses, as they clinked I took a sip. It went down so smoothly, it was fruity and refreshing, delicious.

I smiled at him, "Thank you, Carter."

He put his glass down, "No, thank you for giving me a chance, a chance to try something new."

CHAPTER SEVENTEEN

The weeks were flying since I had been working in my new position, things were going great with Carter and the wedding was literally around the corner.

I was currently working with the new magazines that Cole Enterprises took over a couple of months ago. I was sitting down with the editor of Dream Life Magazine when my phone started ringing, "Sorry, excuse me Dean." I stood up from my seat and walked over to the window, it was Carter. "Hey, is everything okay? I'm just with Dean getting the last bits sorted ready for publishing this Friday?" I smiled as I heard his voice.

"Hey baby, yeah everything is fine. Just wanted to make sure your boss wasn't keeping you too busy," I could hear him smiling, "and to remind you we have dinner tonight with Ava and Mum at 7pm. I will pick you up from yours okay?"

I shook my head, "Of course, I wouldn't have forgotten!" I said.

He knew me well, I had forgotten, "Yeah, that's fine babe, I will see you at seven."

A smirk came onto my face, "See you soon." I walked quickly back over to Dean, "So sorry, where were we?"

After finishing up with Dean, I headed back to our offices. I couldn't believe Laura was getting married in just under two weeks, she had been so calm. To be honest, I thought she would have turned into a bridezilla by now.

I walked into the main reception. It was such a beautiful light space, floor to ceiling glass windows with very minimalistic décor. There were large white leather sofas in the reception area with silver feet sitting off of the high gloss white floor tiles. A long glass coffee table sat in the middle of the sofas, with beautiful plants in the corner. The reception desk was glossed white marble and pristinely dressed employees sat behind it.

I smiled as I walked towards the elevator and went up to my office, "Afternoon Vivienne," I said as I walked into my office. Vivienne was my assistant; she had short chin length blonde hair, blue eyes and was very pretty.

I slumped my old tatty bag down on the floor. *Maybe I should have taken the Louis Vuitton,* I thought. I woke my computer up and started working on my notes from my meeting with Dean. As I was typing up I laughed to myself, this wasn't the job I wanted but I must admit, I was really enjoying my role. There was plenty of writing involved, lots of socialising and I wasn't pining after my failed blog with

You Magazine.

I looked at the clock, 4:45pm, I finished up my recommendations on how Dream Life Magazine would change when we took over, and also noted down the list of notes that Dean wanted me to write up for him.

I was so excited for tonight but nervous as well. I was meeting Carter's mum Elsie and his sister Ava for the first time. I had heard so much about them I felt like I already knew them. As I sat on the train home, my phone buzzed, it was Carter

Can't wait to see you tonight, I will pick you up at 7 xx

I smiled and typed a quick reply. I really did need to message Ethan and see how he was. We had managed to stay friends even though he wasn't best thrilled to see that Carter and I were trying to make it work.

I shook the negative feeling that entered my head. I was seeing Laura tomorrow to have a well needed catch up before the wedding in a couple of weeks.

After a hot, sticky, train ride and a short taxi ride, I was finally home. I walked upstairs and let myself in and headed straight to the bedroom.

I couldn't decide what to wear, I knew we were going to 'Marcus's – at The Berkeley' so I know I needed to dress up but didn't want to overdo it.

I hopped into the shower and washed my hair. I simply didn't want to get out, the warm water hitting my skin felt so refreshing after a long day at the office. The British summer was finally here, the weather had been amazing these last few weeks - the evenings were still warm and enjoyable.

I stepped out of the shower and brushed my teeth then I walked to my wardrobe. After what felt like a lifetime, I decided on a black skater dress. The sleeves were ruffled slightly on the shoulders and it clung to my curves perfectly then as it came to my thighs it flared out slightly. I moisturized my legs and slipped into my Louboutin's, they were so lovely.

I sat on my bed and attempted my make-up. I managed to do a subtle flick on the end of each eye lids, applied my mascara, bronzer and finally settled for a red lipstick. I rough dried my auburn hair before drying and styling it properly. I went for straight hair - it was far too hot to be mucking about with curling tongs.

I reached up to the top of my wardrobe and grabbed my small black shoulder bag. I threw my card, some change, my lipstick, mirror and phone in there. I had one more look in the mirror before walking into the living room. I hadn't realised how short this dress was, it looked even shorter with my heels on.

I pulled a bottle of wine out of the fridge and finished it off while waiting for Carter. I looked at the time: 7pm. I left some food out for Tilly as she was snoozing on the sofa – all she does is sleep.

I was starting to pace the hallway by this time. It was so unlike him to be late, but it was now 7:15 and our table was booked for 7:30. I tried calling him, but he didn't answer.

Then I started panicking, what if something had happened to him? After another five minutes, I heard a knock on my door. I grabbed my clutch off the kitchen side and opened the door, my heart had stopped thumping, it was him. "You're late," I said with a furrowed brow.

He stepped towards me and kissed me on the cheek, "And you're beautiful," he said with a smile.

He smelt so good, his hair was tussled into a messy side parting; he was wearing a dark grey suit with a white shirt slightly opened and black shoes. He looked so handsome. I just could never get over how beautiful this man was, everything about him was perfect.

I locked my front door and we headed to the front door of the apartments. Of course, there James was waiting with the back-door open, a little nod from him wished me a good evening - he was such a nice man. I scooted across so Carter could sit next to me then he took my hand in his and kissed it. "I've bought you a present," he smiled as he reached inside his suit jacket and pulled out a Cartier box.

My heart stopped. He opened it and inside was a beautiful thin diamond bracelet, "Oh Carter, it's so beautiful." He slowly took it out of the box and put it round my right wrist, then fastened the delicate clasp. I shook my wrist gently after watching the light bounce off the diamonds, I looked up at him, "What is this for?" I asked.

He put his hand on my thigh, "For giving me the chance."

I rolled my eyes at him, "I don't need presents Carter, I just need you, and I have that." I leant up and kissed him gently on his lips, his grip tightened on my thigh and his right hand slowly moved to my face as his kiss got deeper. I pulled away, "Hey you, slow down, we will be with your mum and sister soon, I don't want to walk in all hot and flustered, and you now have red lipstick smudged over your lips!"

I laughed then took my mirror out of my clutch and showed him. He pulled a handkerchief out from his pocket and wiped his mouth "What an earth possessed you to wear red lipstick when you knew we would be kissing?" he said with a raised eyebrow.

I smirked "I thought it went well with the dress and shoes," I shrugged.

He placed his handkerchief back into his inside pocket, "Well you were right, it does go well," he said. I took the mirror off of him and touched up my lipstick.

The car pulled up outside The Berkeley. What a beautiful building that was, too - spotlights in the floor, glass panelled porch with well-dressed doormen waiting for us.

James opened the door and Carter stepped out, turning around and taking my hand to help me out of the car. Carter said goodbye to James and he would call him when we were ready.

We walked slowly towards the main door as the doorman smiled and greeted Carter and I, "Good evening Mr Cole, Miss Greene." I blushed, I wasn't used to this, and how did he know my name?

I looked up at Carter, he squeezed my hand as we walked into the lavish reception area. We walked towards the restaurant, butterflies started to hit my belly as we approached our table.

"Evening Mum, Ava," Carter leant in and gave his mum a kiss on the cheek, then walked round to Ava and kissed her too. I stood awkwardly with my legs crossed and clutched onto my bag while I waited for Carter to finish his hellos.

He stood next to me and put his arm around my waist "Mum, Ava, this is Freya."

I smiled at them, "Hi, it's so nice to finally meet you" she smiled down at me then he slowly ran his hand across my back and took my hand. He walked me to the other side of the table and pulled my chair out, "Thank you" I smiled back at him. He then undid his suit jacket and took his seat next to me, still holding my hand.

The waitress came over and poured us all a glass of crisp white wine then placed the bottle back in the cooler.

I watched as Carter spoke to his mother and sister with such respect, he really was a gentleman. "So, Freya, what is it that you do for work?" Elsie asked while taking a sip of her wine. She had dyed brown hair, beautiful green eyes with slight wrinkles either side. She must have been in her late fifties, but she looked immaculate.

She was wearing a Chanel two set ivory suit with open toed sandals. I placed my glass down and knotted my fingers, "I actually work for Carter, I'm a virtual assistant. It's a new role I have been in for the last few weeks." I grinned at her.

She looked puzzled, "A virtual assistant?" she asked.

I went to speak but Carter did it for me, "Yes mum, Freya helps me with the paperwork when I buy a company, she then sits down with the team and sorts out everything legal, social, and any type of writing that the team needs done. She works at numerous offices and is a great asset to the team. She eventually wants to be a writer, so, once she is ready to move on, she can transfer to whichever company she wishes," he squeezed my hand. "She was working for You Magazine before I bought her over to Cole Enterprises as an assistant and also helped out when Sam went on long term sick."

Ava looked at me and smiled "So that's how you two met then?" she asked.

"It was," I said, nodding and smiling back at her.

She pursed her lips, "You are one of the few girls of Carter's we have met, it's lovely to see him with someone again," she said eyeing Carter.

He eyed her back. "Anyway," he chirped in, "let's order, I am starving!"

While Carter was ordering, I studied Ava. She was very

pixie like, little features, same green eyes as Elsie and Carter, her naturally wavy long hair had a slight auburn hint to it, her lips were full, again like Carters. She must have only been a size 6-8, where I'm more of a 10, she was very straight bodied with breasts that seem too big for her delicate frame. Me on the other hand, I'm more of a figure of eight with a little waist. I couldn't help comparing us both.

I was pulled from my thoughts when the waiter asked me what I was having for dinner. After another look at the menu, I decided on Galloway beef. I passed my menu to the waiter, "Thank you, Miss," he grinned and nodded as he walked away. I caught Elsie looking at me, I faced her and smiled at her, "So, Freya, tell us about yourself..." she pursed.

CHAPTER EIGHTEEN

"Okay, that's enough mum," he rolled his eyes "let Freya eat without questioning her on everything..." he said with a scowl.

"Fine, I only want to get to know her a little better," she smiled at me, she had such a kind smile.

"Can we save it for another time? I'm sure you will be seeing Freya again!" he smirked at me, it made my mind wander, maybe he could actually see a future with me, perhaps this was not just a fling.

I know he said he was going to try, but maybe he had realised he didn't want that lifestyle anymore. I quickly shook the thoughts away.

We finished up with dinner and Carter ordered another bottle of wine before he summoned the waiter over and asked for the bill. The waiter quickly returned and nodded as he passed Carter the bill. I watched him as he pulled his wallet out of his inside pocket and gave him a black American express, he didn't even check the amount.

The waiter quickly scurried off to settle the bill, "I can feel you looking at me," he said with a smile.

"You are just too handsome, Mr Cole, I can't keep my eyes of you," I said smiling at him. I put my hand on his thigh and slowly ran my fingers down. He shuffled uncomfortable in his seat, then I remembered we were sitting with his mum and sister.

I quickly retracted my hand and rested and folded my arms on the table before giving them an awkward smile. The waiter returned and gave Carter back his card. He smiled and stood up, doing his suit jacket up, then he walked over to his mum and pulled her chair out, "Thank you dear," she smiled at him, "and thank you for dinner, it was lovely." He then did the same for Ava. She kissed him on the cheek, then he walked over with a smouldering look, he pulled my chair out and took my hand. The electricity sparked through me as we touched.

I stood up and tucked my hair behind my ears. I looked at him, "Thank you so much for dinner," I leant up and kissed him on his cheek, he put his arm around my waist and rested it on the small of my back.

Elsie and Ava walked over to where we were standing, "It was lovely to meet you Freya, Carter seems so happy."

I blushed, "It was lovely meeting you too."

We all walked towards to foyer. All of a sudden, I felt exhausted - it had been a long week. Carter saw his mum and sister out of the hotel and met James at the bottom of the steps, another kiss on the cheek for them both and a warm smile in my direction from Elsie, they stepped into the car and left.

Carter walked back to me, he looked tired too, but he looked good.

"Hey beautiful, did you have a nice night?"

I leant into him, "I always have a good night when I'm with you."

He kissed my forehead, "Let's go to the room," he whispered. I looked at him confused, what did he mean the room?

"Wait, we're not going home?" he shook his head, "I've booked us in for the night here, James has taken my mum and Ava home, and I don't do taxis so I thought it would be a nice treat, a different scenario from the penthouse and townhouse," he smiled, "then I thought we could spend the day together tomorrow. I had my assistant, Sara, buy you a new outfit and underwear for tomorrow, as much as you look breath taking in your dress, I don't think it's suitable for a Saturday chill out."

I smirked at him, "I have to meet Laura tomorrow, remember?"

His face dropped, "Fine, I suppose I can let you go for a couple of hours..." a little smile appeared on his face, he let go of me and walked over to check us in.

He let us into the hotel room, it was just beautiful. He

shut the door and undid the top few buttons of his shirt. It was so nice seeing him relaxed. He walked over to me continuing to undo his buttons, "Let's go shower," he whispered in my ear.

I took his hand, "I would love to shower with you, but I am so tired, I think I will be asleep as soon as my head hits the pillow."

He kissed my hand, "Okay I promise, a quick shower and bed," he winked. I shook my head at him while laughing.

After the shower, I slipped into the silk nighty that Sara had bought. It felt amazing against my skin. I fell into bed while Carter was sitting on his phone answering emails, he looked stressed. "Ahhhh – this bed is amazing," I said while snuggling under the goose feathered duvet. I could have literally lived there, forever.

I looked at Carter and his brows were furrowed, he was rubbing his left hand along his chin.

"What's wrong?" I leant up on my elbows. "Just work stuff babe, one of the companies who we are taking over are not playing ball, so looks like a trip to New York for a few weeks until the dust settles." My heart started beating faster.

"New York? A few weeks?" I didn't want him to go New York, I wanted him to stay here, with me, in London. He locked his phone and rolled onto his side resting his head on his hand as he propped himself up with his elbow, "Freya, it's work, I don't want to go, I need to go."

I looked down at my feet and sighed, "You have lots of

people that can do this for you though Carter."

I didn't know why I had to turned into such a brat, "Because I like to go, I like to meet the directors of the company and for them to feel and realise that we are the right company to take them over, stop being a brat," he smirked at me, "now stop sulking and give me a cuddle." I slid myself over to him and snuggled into his chest, his fingers twirling my hair.

We laid in silence for what seemed like forever when he finally spoke, "Why don't you come with me? I would need you to do some bits anyway, you can work a few days and have the rest as a holiday, that way, we can be together, and I can also keep an eye on you so no one else gets their hands on you."

I leant up and looked at him, shocked and gave him a gentle elbow in the side. He let out a soft laugh and kissed me on the forehead, "I'm only joking," he said as he relaxed back down. I felt a pang of disappointment, maybe this was his way of wanting to cool things off, maybe it was getting boring with me. "I was joking about keeping an eye on you, but totally serious about you coming to New York, I think it would be good for us!" I could feel him looking at me while he was waiting for an answer.

I was still snuggled into his chest staring blankly at the hotel room wall, could I go to New York with him? I sat up and knotted my fingers, then turned to look at him

"I'll think about it, I'll have to sort the cat, I have sort of abandoned her since meeting you," I rolled my eyes. "Plus, we have Laura's wedding, and I can't miss that!" I scoffed. "Then you would probably get sick of the sight of me, how long would we be going for? I know you said a few weeks, but it will be more 1-2 weeks wouldn't it?"

He looked at me bemused, a little smile creeping across his lips, "Have you finished thinking out loud now?" he laughed.

I felt myself blush. I had carried myself away a bit. He scooted across the super king bed and sat next to me, "It would be around 4-6 weeks, dependant on how this company behaves when we get there, I definitely wouldn't be sick of the sight of you Freya. I don't think I could ever get sick of the sight of you, and excuse me, don't blame me for your negligence with Tilly, she's basically moved in with Erin now anyway." He took my hands, "Just think about it, if not, well I suppose we could make it work on a long-distance relationship basis, but I will miss you." He moved my hand up to his lips and kissed it softly.

I smiled at him, he really was wonderful, "Okay, I'll think about it," I leant over and kissed him softly on the lips, his hands tracing my jaw line as our kiss got deeper.

I moved onto my knees in front of him and wrapped my arms around his neck, his hands moved to my hips as he pulled me towards him. I was falling for him so fast, I had never felt like this before. Just as my thoughts trailed off, he pulled away, "That's enough for tonight, I know what you are like. Into bed missy, you're tired."

He was right, I was tired, but I wanted him. "But..."

He looked at me, "no buts." He kissed me on the head and got up and walked into the lounge area of the hotel. I snuggled down into bed and within minutes, I was gone.

I reached over to find Carter was already out of bed. I sat up and checked the time: 09:04am. I felt so rested. I stretched up then got myself out of bed and walked through the double sliding doors of the bedroom and into the lounge area.

Carter was sitting at the end of the dining table reading a newspaper and drinking his Americano. He looked up over his paper with his coffee held up to his mouth and smiled, "Morning beautiful, how did you sleep?" he said taking a sip, I smiled back at him.

"Good morning yourself, I slept amazingly. It was so needed; this week has wiped me."

We were interrupted by a knock on the hotel door, "Oh that's just room service, I realised we have never had a proper breakfast together so, I ordered everything off the menu. I didn't know what you would want."

He got up from the table and opened the door where he greeted the waiter. The waiter pushed a long silver tray with 10 or more silver dishes with lids on and placed it at the side of the table. Carter thanked him and passed him a tip as he walked him out of the room.

I had already started lifting the lids off, there was fruit, cereal, pancakes, waffles, bacon, eggs, toast, breakfast pastries, you name it, it was there.

My mouth was watering. I poured myself a cup of tea and helped myself to some pancakes and bacon, it was really good. "So, I've been thinking," I said after taking a big mouthful of tea, "if I do come to New York, I think we need to know a bit more about each other..."

He looked at me from the other end of the table "What do you mean?" he said raising his eyebrows.

"Well, I don't know when your birthday is, I don't know what music you are into, your hobbies, your friends..."

He pushed his coffee cup along the table and rested his elbows on top of his paper. "My Birthday is 6th May 1985; I like my old school R&B, Motown and Swing; I also like my modern stuff, but I love Kings of Leon. I would probably say they are my all-time favourite. I like golf, not that I'm very good at it, I have a handful of close school friends, we see each other once a month," he smirked at me "is there anything else?"

I just looked at him, "Well, I wasn't expecting you to just answer, I was using them as examples. But no, at the moment there isn't anything else I can think of..." he just laughed at me.

I looked at the time, I really had to get ready to meet Laura. As I stood up I walked over and kissed him on the cheek, "Thank you for all of this Carter, honestly, I am so grateful."

He smiled up at me, "I know baby," he tapped me on the bum, "go get dressed, I will call James."

I walked into the large bathroom, dropped my nightie to the floor, stepped out and walked into the shower. I heard the bedroom door slide open and there he was, my amazing, handsome maybe boyfriend stepped out of his clothes and joining me in the shower.

He stood behind me and wrapped his arms around my waist and snuggled his head into my wet hair, "You smell lovely." He then reached out to get the soap and the sponge and he gently washed my back and moved slowly down to my bum, then he moved the sponge round to the front of my body.

He placed the sponge back on the shelf and kissed my neck, "We don't have time for this now baby, let's get dressed and meet Laura." I rinsed myself off and left Carter to get washed. I was so aroused, but he was right, I didn't want to be late to meet Laura.

I went to the hotel's wardrobe and new clothes were hanging there, a beautiful pale pink chiffon sleeveless shirt, a light pair of jeans and some white havaianas flip flops, folded up underneath was a beautiful lace bra and knicker set. I didn't have a clue what designer the clothes were, I had never heard of them. I got myself dressed and dried my hair with the hairdryer and put what little make up I had in my bag from last night. I was just going to have to go au natural today.

Carter came out of the bathroom and pulled out some jeans, a loose polo shirt and slipped his converse on. I love his casual look, a little bit of wax in his hair giving it the messy tussled look. He walked over the bed side unit and slipped his phone into his back pocket and slid his Rolex onto his wrist, "You look lovely, you ready?" he kissed me on the head.

I nodded.

"Let's go," he said. We left the beautiful hotel room and closed the door behind us.

CHAPTER NINETEEN

I hadn't realised Carter was coming with me, it's wasn't really a problem, but you can't really have a girly chat with your male interest sitting next to you, can you?

We walked into the deli where we used to meet for lunch and sat down at our usual table. Antonio left some menus and gave me a smile while pulling a stupid face behind Carter's back. I shook my head at him.

Last time I was in here, I bumped into Jake and his supposed fiancée. It was so awkward and uncomfortable seeing them together, bringing back all the hurt and memories of our failed relationship.

I was deep in thought when I was interrupted "Freya, baby, is everything okay?"

I shook my head and smiled, "Sorry, just was in deep thought about last time I was here."

I gave him a sympathetic look as he reached over and gently stroked my hand, "His loss, Freya." I was sure this man could read my mind. Then Laura walked in, "Hey, sorry I'm late, oh if I knew men were joining us I would have invited Tyler along," she gave me a look, "anyway, nice to see you Carter."

She squeezed next to me and gave me a kiss on the cheek, Antonio walked over to take our drinks and food order, to be honest I wasn't overly hungry, so I went for a salad.

Carter looked so bored while Laura was talking about the wedding; she was telling me how she was having issues with some of the suppliers and that she wished she had just eloped. "So, Carter, are you joining Freya as her plus one?"

I glared at her. "I haven't actually asked Carter yet Laura," I said shuffling uncomfortably in my seat, he looked at me then darted his eyes to Laura.

"I would love to be Freya's plus one, the timing is perfect. I had an email this morning and I leave for New York on the 19th August, so at least we get a few days together before I have to leave,"

I placed my fork down. "Oh, when did you find that out?" I couldn't help but feel disappointed, I knew he had to go but didn't realise it would be so soon. Laura was looking at me then looking at Carter.

"I found out about an hour ago," he smiled weakly.

I picked my fork back up and put some salad leaves in my mouth and nodded. "Ohhh New York, very fancy! I've always wanted to go New York for the shopping," she said excitedly. Carter smiled warmly at her, "It really is a great place, if you and Tyler can go, then do. I have an apartment there that you could use if you do go."

She beamed at him across the table, "Ah that's lovely Carter, thank you," he looked at me, I was too busy staring down at my boring salad.

"You are welcome," he smiled at Laura.

I changed the subject completely, "I'm going to head up on Wednesday, have a few days with mum and dad. Then will stay with you Thursday night and come home Sunday. Be nice to go home and have a few days chilling."

Laura clapped her hands excitedly, "I can't wait to go back home, have a little sleepover with my bestie the night before the wedding."

I was looking forward to it, I had missed mum and dad so much and even our little village, "I'll come down Wednesday with you Freya, that way we can spend some time together, I can meet your mum and dad and then I will get the train Sunday ready to go to the airport on Monday. If you are coming then we can head up together," said Carter, his eyes were burning into mine. We sat in silence.

"Wait, what, Freya? What the hell, you are thinking of going New York?" she asked abruptly.

"I am thinking about it, yes," I stammered at her.

"What about your job? Tilly? The flat?" she questioned.

"Well, it is technically work," Carter answered for me, "we are in the process of buying a company in New York but the director is being tough, so I am going out there to smooth a few things out and to see if I can get him to sell to me," he said, still smiling. "Freya deals with the new takeovers, so if it is successful I will need her there with me."

I nodded. "And as for Tilly," he said, "Erin is watching her and will check on Freya's apartment while she is away," he signalled Antonio over.

Laura just sat there stunned, staring at me, "Well, if you want to go, then what's stopping you?" Carter paid for lunch; Laura hadn't even noticed.

"Nothing is stopping me, it's just a big decision, I would be gone anything from four to six weeks, it's a long time to be with just him and away from my home comforts."

She nodded, "I understand that hun," she said gently, "but I really do think it would be good for you, and Carter." She smiled at him, "And thank you for lunch Carter, you really didn't have to!"

He smiled back at her, "My pleasure Laura." His phone started ringing, "Excuse me, I have to take this. Laura, it was lovely seeing you, Freya, I will see you outside." He waved at Laura and gave me a wink as he answered his phone and walked out of the deli bar. I watched him walk away and smiled.

"So, what's the reason you don't want to go New York, missy?" Laura pounced on me as soon as he was out of ear shot.

I rolled my eyes at her and sighed, "It's not that I don't

want to go, I really do. I am just scared of getting hurt. Things are going amazingly at the minute and I don't want to risk losing him by going away with him. I know it's for work, and he has said I would only be needed for three days a week and the rest is my time, but it is a big step to take. I never went away with Jake, and to be honest, I'm petrified. I'm worried I will never be enough for him." I knotted my fingers and looked down into my lap.

"Sweetie, you have got to stop comparing Carter to Jake. Jake was a school sweetheart, your first love, it's so rare that those relationships last. I'm not condoning what he done to you, but it was the best thing that happened, especially for you. Look how far you have come. I think the trip to New York would be amazing for you both. If Carter had any concerns about his relationship with you, he wouldn't be asking you. You would be having set up Skype meetings while you are sitting in your office. Have a little faith. I have a good feeling about this one." She put her arm around me, "I know you worry Freya, but don't."

I leant into her, "But we have only been together a few weeks, we are running into something head first. I don't even know that much about him, I only found out his birthday this morning!" I scoffed.

"It's a big step," she nodded and stroked my hair, "I know it is, but it is an amazing big step to take. Sleep on it, you haven't got to decide just yet, let him know on the day we go down to Elsworth."

I nodded, "Yeah, I will, come on, he will be waiting."

We said bye to Antonio and headed to the street where Carter was already sitting in the car. I hugged Laura goodbye and we gave each other a kiss on the cheek. "This time next week you will be married!" I squealed with excitement.

"Oh yeah, oh wow that is a scary thought!" she said beaming, "but so exciting, too!" she said in a high pitch voice. We laughed and said our last goodbyes, Carter offered her a lift but she refused, saying she was meeting Tyler up the road to go through some last bits then she waved to Carter and walked off down the street.

James shut the door after me as I slid in next to Carter, "Thank you for lunch," I said giving him a kiss on the cheek.

"You are most welcome," he replied giving my hand a squeeze "where did you want to go now?" he asked.

"Back to my place?" I said as a pang of excitement went through me.

"Sounds perfect – I've missed you," he gave me a hungry look.

"What do you mean miss m...?" I blushed. "Oh, I understand," I smiled at him.

"James, can you drop us to Freya's please?" he asked so politely, he really does have respect for his employees and I love that about him. We sat silently, looking out the window when all of a sudden, I was distracted by Carter, his hand was slowly moving between my thighs. "I can't wait to get you home," he whispered in my ear, as he started kissing my neck. He pulled away and gently kissed me on the lips, his kiss was slow but hard, his tongue exploring my mouth, my hands moved up to his hair, slowly running and gently tugging at his messy hair. He pulled me onto his lap as his kiss got more heated. I wanted him here, now, but we couldn't.

I pulled away from him, "Stop, we will be home soon. James is there!" I looked over my shoulder nervously, waiting to have James's eyes meet mine in the rear-view mirror.

Carter turned my head back round gently, "He wouldn't even notice, trust me," he said moving back in for a kiss, "plus, I wouldn't want to make love to you in the back of a car Freya, I want to take you home."

I blushed at the thought.

"Anyway, not too much longer to wait, we are nearly at yours now," he smiled at me, and before I knew it, we were kerbside outside the apartments. "James, I will speak to you later, don't hang around," James nodded and said goodbye.

We walked into the apartment block and up to my apartment. I rummaged around in my bag to find my keys and opened the door. I kicked my flip flops off and dumped my bag on the worktop. I turned around to face Carter when he swooped me up and put me on the kitchen side, standing in between my thighs.

"You are so beautiful Freya; how did I get so lucky?"

I took his hands into mine, "I wouldn't say you were

lucky, I'm the lucky one." I kissed his hands gently, "Honestly, I am, the luckiest girl in the world." I smiled at him.

"Well let's just agree to disagree shall we?" he said as he smirked at me and slowly moved down to kiss me.

He slowly unbuttoned my pink chiffon shirt and slowly slid it down my arms and throwing it on the sofa behind me. He kissed down my neck and along my collar bone, my hands were round his back as I started to peel his white t-shirt off, he pulled away as I lifted his t-shirt over his head.

He came back towards me kissing me deeply. I could lose myself in this man again and again. I slid off the kitchen side and stood in front of him undoing his jean buttons, before I could pull them down he picked me up and carried me to the bedroom.

He gently dropped me onto the bed and crawled up over me, he undid my jeans and slid them down my legs, slowly crawling back over me and kissing me. His fingers slowly made their way to my sweet spot, circling and teasing before slowly sliding them in, his mouth still on mine kissing me, his tongue mirroring the rhythm of his fingers.

I was building too fast, "Stop, stop, please."

He slowly slid his finger out, "What's wrong?" he asked concerned.

"Nothing, I just don't want to be over so quick," I muttered, trying to catch my breath.

"Don't worry about that, you'll still enjoy every

moment," he said, smirking at me.

He took his boxers off and hovered over me, "Turn over," he said. I did as he said and turned over. I felt exposed. I felt him kneel behind me as his hands slowly moved round my hips; before I could say anything, he put himself inside of me. He started moving slowly but hard, it felt so good.

I had a dull ache low in my belly as he was moving in and out of me, the sensation building, my hips started moving with him, making him groan. He sped up, I could feel my orgasm getting close as he moved faster and harder, "Carter, please, keep going," as soon as the words were out my mouth I climaxed around him with him following me.

We lay in bed next to each other, chatting about this week's work. I only had to go in for two days as I was off on Wednesday to go back to Elsworth. I couldn't wait to go back home, but I wasn't looking forward to the memories that came with it, but hopefully having Carter with me it would make it a lot easier. I was looking forward to him meeting my mum and dad and seeing where I grew up.

I hadn't told him yet, but I was going to go New York, Laura was right, I didn't want to miss this opportunity and I did think it would do wonders for me and Carter.

"What are you thinking about?" he asked while stroking my arm.

"Not a lot, Elsworth next week, the wedding, New York..." I could feel him looking at me.

"New York? Really?" he sounded like an excited

schoolboy.

"Yes, really," I looked up at him and smiled, "I can't wait!"

He leant down and kissed me, "I'm so happy you are coming with me!" he rolled over on top of me, "Round two?" he asked with a smirk. I laughed at him before losing myself in him.

CHAPTER TWENTY

Carter and I spent the rest of the weekend with each other, flitting between another's apartments. I stayed at his on Sunday and we went to work together.

I was quite glad we only had two more days at work before going to see my mum and dad, ready for Laura and Tyler's wedding. I couldn't believe how quickly it had come around.

I said bye to Carter and went into my office, I do like to try and keep it professional at work. I turned my computer on and spent most the morning going through my emails. We had just taken over a shipping yard in York, so I had a few details to tie up with Mr Burns before we left for Elsworth.

My assistant had sent me the flight details for New York - we were leaving Monday morning, the 21st. It wasn't until we sat down and went through the days that I realised we are out there for my birthday, what a way to bring in your 29th. My birthday is the 22nd September so I was sure Carter would arrange something while we are out there. I printed our boarding passes off and put them into my bag, I was getting excited now.

Before I knew it, I was shutting my computer off for the last time for a few weeks. I met Carter downstairs and gave him a soft kiss on the lips, "Hey you," I smiled at him, "did you have a good day?" I asked.

He held me round my waist as we walked over to the car, "I had a very good day, but I must admit, I am really looking forward to the next few days."

I beamed as we got into the car.

We really needed to pack tonight, so we agreed that we would both stay at our own places so we could back and do what we needed to do.

We pulled up to my apartment, I leant over and kissed Carter goodbye. It was only a night, but I was really going to miss him.

"See you tomorrow, I'll miss you."

He kissed me back hard, resting his hand on my cheek. "I'll miss you more, I will see you tomorrow. Be ready for 10am." I smiled and left the car then I stood on the pavement and watched him drive away.

I felt sad, we had been spending so much time together, what with work and the weekends, it felt weird not being with him. I let myself into the apartments and checked my post box. As I was looking through the letters, Ethan appeared, "Hey stranger!"

I looked up at him "Ethan!" I threw my arms round his neck and hugged him, "How are you?" I asked.

"Er, yeah I'm ok thanks, how about you?" he stepped back and smiled.

Maybe I shouldn't have hugged him. "Yeah, I'm ok, leaving for Elsworth in the morning. We have Laura's wedding this Friday and then I'm leaving for New York on Monday for a few weeks for work."

He looked shocked, "Wow, New York! That's great Freya, when are you home?"

I tucked my hair behind my ear, "Beginning of October I think, unless I can get things tied up before that, but that's when my flight is booked for."

He put his hand round the back of his head and rubbed it, "Wow, that's a long time. I assume you are going with Carter?" his lips pursed into a thin line.

"Yeah, I am," I gave him a weak smile.

I do sometimes wonder what me and Ethan would have been if I had never met Carter. We did get on well, and he is such a sweetheart, but it just wasn't meant to be. He broke my trail of thought, "Anyway, I will let you go, you are super busy. Give me a text, don't be stranger, maybe we can grab a drink when you are back?" he placed his hands in his pockets and rocked slightly back and forth on the balls of his feet.

"Sure! I'll look forward to it!" I replied, "take care Ethan, see you soon." I gave him one last smile before going into the apartment.

Tilly was nowhere to be seen, but to be honest, it'd been like this for a while now and Erin likes having her anyway. Once I'm back home I will get her settled again back here.

I walked through the door and straight to the fridge, I had nothing in. I made a quick call and ordered myself a pizza, then I thought I better call my mum to let her know what time we were hoping to be there.

It rang a few times before she answered, "Hello," she talks so posh on the phone.

"Hey! Mum! It's Freya"

"Harry, quick, it's Freya!"

I don't think she realises only one person can talk on the house phone; I could hear my dad muttering in the background.

"Hey mum, was just calling to let you know that me and Carter are leaving at ten tomorrow morning, I've just checked and it says we should be there by about eleven thirty, dependant on traffic of course."

I heard her squeal to my dad, "Harry, did you hear that, she's bringing her rich boyfriend Carter to stay!"

I then heard my dad telling her to set the spare room up as he wasn't allowed in my bedroom. I laughed to myself, he is so old school.

"Anyway, Mum, you still there?"

"Oh yes darling, still here. Well drive safely, I will have the tea and sandwiches ready for you and Carter. Keep me updated with the traffic dear!"

"I will mum, I will speak to you tomorrow, love you-"

"Yes darling, love you," she replied. As I went to put the phone down, I heard her telling Dad how excited she was that I was coming up and she was looking forward to meeting Carter.

I headed to the bedroom and stood in front of my wardrobe, not only did I have to pack for Elsworth, I also had to pack for over a month's travel to New York.

Carter had told me not to go mad as he would buy me a new wardrobe out there, but I didn't want him to do that. I had my own money and my own clothes to take.

I decided to sort the bits for home first, packing a couple of pairs of jeans, t-shirts, shirts, a handful of underwear and a couple of pairs of shoes.

I was pretty sure I still had stuff back home, and also my mum is a washing ninja, as soon as something was in the wash basket, it was back on your bed washed and ironed within an hour. I really don't know how she does it. I heard the intercom go and answered, finally the pizza was here. I thanked the driver and walked back into my bedroom, eating as I packed.

I heard my phone buzz, I searched through the pile of clothes to find it and smiled as I checked the screen, it was Carter:

Hey Beautiful, really missing you. I can't wait to see you tomorrow, I just wanted to say I've really enjoyed these last few weeks. Hope the packing Is going well, text me before bed, C xx

I typed a quick reply back to him and threw the phone back on the bed. I was getting so excited, back home, Laura's wedding and New York. I'm pretty sure nothing could burst my bubble. I put my little suitcase by the door ready for Elsworth and went back into the bedroom to start packing for New York. It was going to be a long night.

I looked at the time, eleven pm, that wasn't too bad. I stripped off and stepped into my shower washing my hair so all I had to do in the morning was wash and get dressed.

I stood there thinking about how things were going with Carter, and if he really was happy with the situation, whether deep down he was missing how his life used to be.

I supposed it had only been a few weeks, and that we were still in the 'honeymoon' period as they call it. *I've got to stop overthinking it and live in the moment,* I thought to myself. It's going good now, so there's no point worrying what is going to happen in the future, we are both happy.

I washed the shampoo out of my hair and applied the conditioner. I really need to get a cut when I get home. I stepped out of the shower and brushed my teeth. Then, I found an old t-shirt and shorts and threw them on. I pulled my old mirror and propped it up on my bed while I dried my hair.

I looked over at my New York suitcase, I was really doing this, I was so nervous but excited at the same time. *It's going to be amazing Freya*, I told myself.

I put all the clothes away that I decided not to take and made my way through the flat cleaning so it was all done for when I was home. I bagged the rubbish up and left that by the front door, I will throw that out in the morning.

I turned the lights off and locked the door and climbed into bed, it was quarter past midnight by the time I had finished. I gave Carter a quick text - I doubted he would be awake, he had probably been in bed since nine, seeing as he has housekeepers to look after him. *How the other half live*, I smiled, that's something my dad's mum would always say. I plugged my phone in and set a reminder on my phone for me to remember my charger. I opened my messages and text Carter:

Hey, you, just got into bed. I'm missing you, feels weird spending a night without you seeing as we have lived in each other's pockets for the last few weeks. I bet you are fast asleep, I am all packed and bags ready at the door. See you tomorrow, Night xx

I put my phone back on the table when I heard it buzz, of course it was him:

Night baby, I said I wanted you to text me before bed, so I stayed up. See you in the morning, C xx

I smiled and rolled over. I really felt like the luckiest woman in the world. I got myself comfortable and within minutes I was asleep.

I rolled over and looked at the time, eight am. I groaned, I felt so groggy this morning, I had a hectic day yesterday tying up the loose ends at work, and then a late-night packing two bags for this weekend and my time in New York.

I lay in bed for about fifteen minutes as I struggled to get myself going. When I finally did decide to leave my amazing bed, I shuffled over to the kitchen and flicked the switch on the kettle. I needed tea.

I shuffled back into my bedroom and into the bathroom, as I got up I caught a glimpse of myself in the mirror, my god, I looked horrendous.

I turned the bathroom light off and went back into the kitchen to pour myself a cup of tea. I sat on the sofa, in complete silence listening to the birds outside. I take the sound for granted really. Once my tea was finished, I rinsed the cup and left it on the draining board, then headed back into the bedroom to get myself dressed.

I decided on a light grey summer dress and my faithful flip flops, the weather man said it was going to be a warm one today, and by weather man, I mean the app on my phone.

I ran the straighteners over my hair to try and tame it, applied some concealer under my god-awful bags then gave myself a light dusting of bronzer and a flick of mascara. That'd do. I checked my bags again, making sure I had everything. I then picked up my phone charger and popped that into my weekend bag.

Finally, I walked over to my bedside cabinet and picked up my passport and put that in my New York suitcase. I was feeling so anxious now, anxious to be going back home. I haven't been home since me and Jake ended, the house sale was all done via Skype and emails – I literally had no reason to go back, apart from mum and dad obviously, but I knew I would be seeing them for the wedding. What if I bumped into him and Aimee? Even thinking her name made me feel nauseous. It'd be fine, I would have Carter.

I looked at the time, nine forty-five, I quickly ran back through the flat to make sure everything was off, the straighteners had cooled down now so I unplugged them and wrapped them up and placed on my suitcase. I ran back into the bedroom and turned all my switches off and then decided to have one more wee 'for the journey'.

I walked into the lounge area and waited for Carter, I rammed my straighteners into the suitcase – I really didn't want to forget them. Bang on ten, Carter knocked at the door. I opened it with a big smile on my face as he stepped into the apartment and wrapped his arms around me, lifting me off the floor. My arms were tight round his neck as he planted a kiss on my lips. "God I missed you Freya," he said into my hair.

I buried my head into his neck "I missed you, too," I whispered.

He put me down gently and took my bags, "Freya what have you packed?" he said, strained, "these are ridiculous, do you need this much? I said I would buy you new clothes when we get to New York."

I rolled my eyes at him, "Oh hush will you, just take the bags Cole," I said laughing, "by the way, your bum looks lovely in those chinos." It really did, he was wearing dark beige chinos, with a white Ralph Lauren polo shirt and boat shoes. He always looked and smelled amazing.

After a struggle, we finally got to the car. Carter moaned the whole time from the apartment to the car. But it really was a gorgeous day.

I was stunned not to see James standing outside, instead what was there was Carter's Maserati, the graphite grey paintwork shone in the sunshine, the beige leather looked rich against the grey. "Erm, babe, are the bags going to fit in the boot?" I giggled; it didn't look like they were going to fit.

"They're going to have to, aren't they?" he said sarcastically. Honestly, he was such a child when he got into these little moods.

I got into the passenger side of the car, it was even more beautiful on the inside as it was on the outside. I put my bag down by my feet and put my sun glasses on. Five minutes, later Carter slid into the driver's seat, red faced and sweaty. He just looked at me and shook his head. He started up the car and the engine roared, it sounded amazing.

Before we set off, he put my mum and dads address in the sat nav then plugged his phone in, the car started playing Usher – 82701 album; this was a favourite of mine. "You ready, beautiful?" he placed his hand on my thigh.

I nodded at him smiling, "Let's go."

He smiled back. He looked over his right shoulder and indicated as he pulled away from the apartments, here we go. Off on our little adventure – and now, I couldn't wait.

CHAPTER TWENTY-ONE

It was such a lovely car ride up to my parents, we spoke most of the way, we talked about what we liked and disliked, our interests, our dreams and ambitions, family and friends.

I felt a pang of anxiety as we started driving down the lanes towards home. Carter could sense this and squeezed my hand, "I'm really looking forward to meeting your family and to see where you grew up." He gave me a sympathetic smile, "it will be fine, Freya." I knew he was right, but when anxiety takes over it takes me a while to shake it. I looked out of the window at the familiar surroundings. It was so nice to see acres and acres of green and farmland - it was nice to be home. Away from the hustle and bustle of London, I love London, but not as much as I loved home. If I were to ever have a family, I would move back there or somewhere like Elsworth. We were lucky to grow up here.

Carter slowed down as we approached my parents beautiful detached cottage, it was like a dream house. Perfect white picket fence around the cottage, a bright pretty flower garden, a cobbled garden path, it was just picture perfect. Carter pulled onto their driveway, the engine made a loud noise as it was switched off.

My parents must have heard the noise from Carter's car as my mum came running down the cobbled path to greet us "Harry! Harry!" she shouted, "Our baby's home, she's home!" she squealed with excitement.

"Rose, stop shouting for goodness sake, the whole village can hear you!" he shouted from the front door then he walked slowly down the path with a big smile on his face.

My dad was 5"9, stocky, mousy brown hair and glowing olive skin with sage eyes. My mum was 5"5, auburn hair, petite but curvy in the right places and beautiful, deep blue eyes. She ran towards me and hugged me so tight, "Oh darling, I've missed you!" she said, tears welling in her eyes. She was kissing me all over my face while holding my head in her hands.

"Rose let go of her, let her breathe!" my dad said sternly, as he moved her aside.

"Ahh my baby face," he said in a softened voice as he hugged me and kissed me on the forehead, "we have missed you sweetheart" he said, giving me a dazzling smile. He then looked over to Carter who had just unloaded the car. "You must be Carter," he said in a stern voice.

"That's correct sir, it's a pleasure to meet you Mr Greene," he held his hand out and shook my dad's. My dad nodded at him and walked over to the suitcases, while having a cheeky look at his car.

My mum had hugged and given Carter a kiss on the cheek and was ushering him into the cottage. He looked over his shoulder and smiled, I shrugged at him and followed dad up the cobble path.

As promised, the tea was on the table served in mum's finest china, biscuits piled up on a dessert plate and fresh finger sandwiches. She had really gone to town for Carter. It was lovely seeing my mum and dad happy and smiling and was also just as lovely seeing Carter relaxed.

As we sat down at the table earlier, he put his phone on silent and put it in my bag; my dad is big on manners and I know that would have meant a lot to him and me, of course.

After our lunch, mum showed us to our bedrooms. I was in my old room and Carter was in the spare down the end of the corridor. He smiled at me as my mum showed him around and told him that under my dad's orders he is to stay in this room. We both laughed and Carter nodded and said he would respect my father's wishes.

I was unpacking when my mum walked in, "Oh Freya, it's so lovely to have you home. Makes us realise how much we have missed you!" she started getting teary again.

"I know mum, I have missed you both too."

She started helping me unpack; tutting at my screwed up and creased clothes "Really, Freya, do you not own an iron?" I rolled my eyes, I had been here just over an hour and she had already started. Once my mum had finished her lecture, I slid the suitcase under the bed "I like Carter," she said out of the blue, "very handsome young man, very respectful, such a gentleman."

I smiled at her, "He really is wonderful, mum," I said sitting down on my bed.

"Where did you meet him?" she asked, sitting herself next to me on the bed.

"I met him at work, mum, I work for him, for his company. I started off helping out when someone went on long term sick, he then headhunted me from the magazine and now I work for him, sort of like a freelance position helping with the admin and writing side of it."

She looked at me confused. "Right, well, you know they say, you shouldn't mix business with pleasure!" and gave me 'the look.'

I could feel myself blush, "Mother!" I exclaimed, "honestly!"

She stood up off the bed and shook her head, "I'm just saying dear, it never normally works out, just be careful." I couldn't believe her, I hope Carter couldn't hear this conversation, and as if she could read my mind she continued, "Don't worry sweetie, your dad has taken Carter down the local pub to meet his friends, he seems very keen on him." He'd taken him to the local, oh I hoped they didn't bring up the drama of Jake and I - that's all he wanted to listen to.

I walked downstairs and put the kettle on, I needed a cup of tea. I'm glad that dad liked Carter but then there wasn't really anything to dislike about him other than his history with his flavours of the month. I scowled at the thought.

Mum came in a little while after and was pottering about in the kitchen, I sat on the sofa and enjoyed the quiet while dad's swing music played subtly in the back ground.

I started thinking about how perfect Laura's wedding was going to be, all the months of planning and saving for their one big day, it really was going to be something special.

I was distracted by the sound of mum talking to herself. I looked over at her and she was in her own little world unloading the dishwasher, I smiled at her.

Just as I drifted back off in my thoughts Carter walked through the door with my dad, they seemed to be laughing with one another, "Go take a seat son, I will grab us a beer from the garage." He slapped Carter on the back and headed for the garden.

Carter came and sat next to me and gave me a kiss on the cheek. "Hey, all okay?" he asked with a silly smile on his face.

I smiled back at him, "All fine here thanks, what about you?"

He nodded, "Yup all good, I love it here. Why did you ever want to move away?"

I rolled my eyes at him, "You know why Mr Cole!" It was

funny seeing him giddy, "how many have you had?"

"Only a couple...." he replied giving me a wink, *oh it'd started already.*

Shortly after, dad came in with a crate of Fosters. He sat in his armchair and put the tins on the coffee table, "I bought these just for you Carter, you know, what with you being an Aussie and all that!"

"Dad!"

"What? He is an Aussie, aren't you Carter?"

Carter laughed at him, "That I am! Cheers!" they clunked their tins together and got lost in conversation about cricket.

After a few hours of chilling, I decided to go to my room and fire up my laptop, I thought I would check in on my emails, make sure everything was okay.

As I scrolled I saw an email from Jools, I smiled as I opened it. She had emailed me to let me know she was stepping down as editor of 'You Magazine' and wanted to wish me good luck for the future and that she had enjoyed working with me. I typed a quick reply asking where she was off to and wishing her well in her new plans. If it wasn't for her, I would never have met Carter. I know she could be a bit of a dragon, but she was okay, deep down.

I was interrupted by a knock on my bedroom door "Hey, only me," Carter said as he walked into my room.

"Hey – I just had an email from Jools, my old editor, letting me know she's stepping down."

He sat down next to me on my bed, "Yeah I heard about that, her husband isn't very well so she's focusing on him at the moment and not the magazine. I told her that her job will be there for her, if she decides to come back."

I looked back the email, I felt insensitive now asking what she was moving onto, "That's nice of you," I muttered. I closed my laptop lid down, "Thought I would just check in, you know, see if everyone is okay without me," I shrugged, it seemed they were.

He moved closer to me, "You are on holiday, enjoy. We have people overseeing your job, just relax."

I smiled, "I am trying," I flopped back on the bed and stared at the ceiling and sighed, "it feels weird being in my old room."

He flopped down beside me, "I bet, I wish I still had my first room from Australia," he mumbled.

I looked sideways to look at him, "I bet you have some good memories from there." I reached for his hand, he faced me and smiled, then leant in and kissed me on the nose.

"Oh, what I would do to you if we were alone," he whispered, my belly tightened, the thought of not being able to have him made me want him more.

I lifted his left arm up and snuggled into his chest, he wrapped his arm round me as we lay there, in complete silence.

I felt myself wake with a jump, I looked at the time- four thirty; we must have dozed off. I looked round, disorientated to see Carter still sound asleep. I slowly got up and crept downstairs to get a drink, as I walked into the lounge Mum and Dad were nowhere to be seen. I walked into the kitchen to find a note:

Freya,

Gone for dinner in the village, did not want to wake either of you. If you want to join us, give me a call.

Love Mum XX

To be honest, I was hungry. I gave her a call on her mobile to see where she was. After a few rings, she answered, "Hello?"

"Mum, it's me, where are you?"

"Who?" I rolled my eyes, "Freya, mum, it's Freya - who else calls you mum?!"

"Well I don't know do I? We are at Bella's the Italian, in the village. Come and meet us, we've just ordered another bottle of wine!"

I laughed, "Okay, I will wake Carter and meet you there." I put the phone down, she sounded pissed.

I walked back upstairs quietly and laid on top of Carter, planting gentle kisses along his chin. He started to stir, "Hey, handsome," I said as he opened his eyes, looking around the room, "nice sleep?" I asked.

Hhe reached up and stretched, "It was a mighty fine sleep," he mumbled.

I sat up on his lap and looked down at him, "So mum and dad have gone for an Italian in the village and want us to meet them down there."

He smiled, "Sounds fab, I'm starving," he said, he went to move but I pinned his arms down to the bed and shook my head, "we've got the house to ourselves."

I leant down and kissed him slowly, teasing him with my tongue. He tried to move his hands, but I pushed down harder. I smiled as I was kissing him, he mirrored my grin, "What about what your dad said? I respect what he asked baby!"

I could feel him growing underneath me. "I know you do," I purred, "but we wouldn't be long, plus they aren't here..."

I let go of his hands and placed them on his stomach, slowly pushing his t-shirt up his body. His hands moved to my hips then slowly down my thighs as he pushed my dress up around my waist, I went up on my knees while I undid his belt and jeans as he slid them down his legs. I slowly removed his boxers, watching him with hungry eyes.

He took a deep breath as he moved my knickers to the side and put his hands back on my waist, slowly moving me down onto him. It felt amazing, we slowly matched each other's rhythm, mirroring each other's moves. His hands were moving up to my breasts as I started to pick up the pace, his breathing started getting heavier as did mine. He then sat up and wrapped his arms around my waist with his head resting against mine as we both started our climb to climax, just as we lost ourselves in each other, he kissed me hard as I moaned into his mouth on my release.

We freshened up and took a slow walk through the village to the Italian restaurant. It was weird walking through these little streets with Carter, hand in hand. Jake and I never did anything like that.

We walked into the restaurant and saw mum and dad sitting at a table in the far corner; mum noticed us and started frantically waving. I smiled at the waiter and walked over to the table, "Hey," they smiled as we sat down.

The wine was flowing, the food was delicious, and the company was great, I couldn't wait for the next few days, especially spending them with Carter.

CHAPTER TWENTY-TWO

Thursday evening was soon upon us. Carter and I had had a lovely few days together, we explored the village, ate good food and even had a date night with Laura and Tyler.

I was upstairs getting my bits together to head over to Laura's parents' house for the evening. They lived a short walk up further into the village.

I heard footsteps coming up the stairs, and there, in the door way, was Carter. He walked over to me and gave me a kiss on the cheek, "I'm going to miss you tonight, it's weird not staying with you in my own house, but to sleep here with your mum and dad while you are at Laura's feels really weird," he let out a laugh.

"I know, it is weird, totally understand if you want to go into a bed and breakfast," I looked at him as a faint smile appeared on his face.

"No baby, I want to stay here, it's only one night. Next time I will be seeing you is you walking down the aisle."

I froze, that sounded strange: imagine Carter and I getting married, him standing in the distance at the altar, while I walked down the aisle towards the man I was falling head over heels in love with.

"I can't wait," he said as he leant down and kissed me on the lips, "do you need help packing anything?" he asked me.

I shook my head, "I'm basically done I think." I looked around the room, "Laura has my dress and accessories. I have packed pjs, toiletries and bits like that so yeah, I think I'm done." I smiled at him.

He walked over and picked my little suitcase up and walked it downstairs for me and left it by the front door. "Thank you," I said.

He smiled back at me.

"So, what are you doing tonight?" I asked him.

"Me and your dad are going to the pub, then I think your mum is meeting us down there once she is back from book club so we can all have dinner."

I loved that he was so respectful with my family, I was a little bit bummed that I would be missing out to be honest, "Sounds nice, I'm jealous."

He smirked at me, "Come on, I will walk you to Laura's."

I laughed, "Honestly, it's okay, you'll get lost!"

He looked to the side and sighed, "I won't get lost, worst comes to worst, I will put your mum and dad's address in my phone."

I nodded. I said bye to my dad and told him I would call them later and see them tomorrow at the venue.

Carter opened the front door for me and picked up my suitcase, "After you," he said as I walked past him. He pulled the door shut behind me and took my hand into his as we walked towards Laura's parents' house.

"I'm really looking forward to New York, thank you for giving me this opportunity."

He rubbed his thumb over the back of my knuckles. "I'm glad you are coming too, I can't wait." It was so nice seeing the softer side of him. I flashed back to the moment I saw him in Jools's office - he used to make me feel so intimidated.

It was a warm evening, people were busy with friends and families were enjoying the sunshine. Summer has to be my all-time favourite season, everyone is so much happier when the sun is shining.

We arrived outside Laura's parent's townhouse. They had a big lawn out front with a large blossom tree sitting pretty to the right of the house, hanging from its branches, was a handmade swing that Gary, Laura's dad, made for us one summer. I watched as it slowly swung in the summer breeze. I smiled watching it, it bought back all of the memories where we our imagination would come to life under that tree. We always had our 'dream' weddings under there, taking it in turns to be the bride.

I really hoped she had some photos under it tomorrow. I opened the picket gate and walked up to their lavish home.

Laura's parents, Gary and Lucinda, had money - they always had. Laura always had the nicest clothes and toys, they always had new cars and their home was immaculate. They were such a generous and warm family and you wouldn't think they came from a wealthy upbringing.

I rang the doorbell and squeezed Carter's hand, within seconds Laura swung the front door open and screamed a high pitch squeal. Carter winced as the scream pierced through our ears. He put his finger in his ear and gave it an itch, "Anyone would think she was excited!" he teased.

She then came bounding out of the door and threw our arms round us both singing at the top of her lungs 'I'm getting married in the morning.'

After finally letting us go and watching her jump up and down on the door step for five minutes, she welcomed us into her home. Gary and Lucinda came into the grand hallway area, "Freya. Sweetheart!" I heard Lucinda call, "Oh it's been so long!" She gave me a hug and a kiss on the cheek, following behind her was Gary who came over and gave me a kiss on the cheek. They were like my second family growing up.

Gary and Lucinda introduced themselves to Carter. I watched them as Laura skipped away into the kitchen, no doubt to get a bottle of champagne. Gary placed his arm around Carter's shoulders and walked him into their lounge. I smiled as they walked off.

I was right, there she came skipping down the hallway with a bottle of Dom Pérignon champagne and two glasses,

"Let's get druunnnk!" she shouted.

Lucinda tutted at her, "I don't think so Laura, you have a wedding to be at tomorrow!" She shook her head, "Don't be so stupid!" she sighed and walked off into the kitchen.

I took my bags up to Laura's room and unpacked everything I needed for tonight. All of a sudden, I heard Carter saying his goodbyes, explaining that he was spending the evening with my parents.

I ran out of Laura's room and down her spiral staircase, I would have slid down the bannister like old times, but to be honest I didn't think it would have held my weight. I got to the bottom step and threw myself at him while planting a soft kiss on his lips, "See you tomorrow," he said quietly, his warm breath on my face.

"I'll miss you," I replied.

He moved in to give me one more kiss, "Now go have fun, text me before you go to sleep, and no getting drunk!"

I rolled my eyes. Lucinda was nodding in agreement with him.

He let me go and walked towards the door, "Gary, Lucinda, it was a pleasure meeting you. Gary, next time you are in town let me know and we will have that game of golf!"

He smiled, "I'm sure I can help you," Gary thanked him and shook his hand. Lucinda gave him a peck on the cheek "Enjoy your evening ladies," he waved up at Laura who was hanging over the bannister.

"Bye Carter!" she shouted down, and he laughed at her.

He then looked at me, "See you later baby," he winked and walked out of the door, closing it softly behind him.

Damn, I missed him already, I was falling far too fast for my liking.

A few hours later, everything had started to calm down. Laura was showered and her hair was washed ready for tomorrow. Our outfits were hanging in Laura's dressing room, all pristine. Our shoes sat neatly at the bottom of our dresses.

I looked at them, all different lengths and shapes. I felt a bit sad that Brooke and Zoe weren't here having a sleepover with us, but it was also nice to just chill.

I was hoping that Laura didn't turn into a bridezilla in the morning as the girls were getting here for nine am. I topped our champagne up and fell onto her bed. "So, are you excited for tomorrow?" A stupid question I know, but it seemed appropriate to ask it.

She rolled over on her belly and beamed at me, "So excited!" she kicked her legs in excitement, "I can't wait to marry him tomorrow, we have been planning this for nearly a year, it's going to be perfect..."

"It really will be. I have been looking forward to this for so long. I get to see my beautiful best friend get married!" I could feel the tears starting to prick my eyes.

She pulled herself along the bed and hugged me, "I'm so glad we are doing this together, there is no one else I would rather have by my side then my Frey Frey!" We laughed together.

I held up my glass, "A toast!" I smiled, "To my beautiful best friend, who is starting her new adventure with her soon to be husband. I love you so much!"

She started to well up, "I love you too," she replied.

"Cheers!" we both said with raised voices and took a big gulp of champagne.

"Now time for facemasks!" she said as she ran towards her en-suite

Half an hour later, we were sitting in her bed, eating chocolate and Doritos with our facemasks on. Laura got her phone out and asked me for a selfie, "Quick snap chat, snap chat!"

I groaned, "Come on, then!"

We pulled a few silly faces and were crying with laughter at some of the filters.

We went to the en-suite and washed our faces –we had definitely had it on a bit too long. I shouted out from the bathroom saying I was going to jump in the shower and wash my hair, "No problem babe! I'm going to binge on Sex and The City!" she shouted back.

I stepped into the shower and let the hot water run over me, it felt so good. I washed my hair. Luckily, I was freshly waxed so no need for last minute shaving.

I stepped out and wrapped myself in the towels, they were so soft, my towels never felt this soft. I made a mental note to ask Lucinda or Mum how to rectify this. *What is wrong with me I am thinking about how soft these towels are,* I thought to myself. I shook my head and got dried and slipped my pjs on then I walked back into the bedroom, "Hun, I am just going to dry my hair."

I looked over at the bed and saw that Laura was sound asleep. I smiled, bless her. She needed a good sleep ready for tomorrow. I walked over and switched the tele off then I walked over to the bed and laughed. I took the bag of crisps out of her hands and tucked her in.

I walked out of the bedroom and into the guest room so I could dry my hair. I was distracted when Lucinda walked in, "Is everything okay?" she asked.

I nodded, "Yeah, fine, I was in the shower and when I walked back out Laura was asleep. I didn't want to wake her so came into here so I could dry my hair."

"Not a problem darling - I'm surprised she kept going as long as she did. She was up at the crack of dawn!" she smiled, "go and get yourself to bed, I will get you both up in the morning."

"See you in the morning," I replied. I walked out of the bedroom and climbed into bed next to Laura.

I picked my phone up and text Carter, it was eleven pm. I typed a quick message, I felt bad that I had left him with my mum and dad and not even text him. Literally as I pressed send he called me.

"Hello," I answered sheepishly.

"Hey you, you ok?" he asked.

"I am now I have heard from you," I smiled into the phone, "how was dinner? Are my parents ok? I was meant to call them, but it has been so hectic."

"It's fine, they understand. Dinner was lovely, it's a really nice pub,"

Bless him, I thought to myself.

"Guess what though!"

My nerves kicked in, oh no what's happened? "What?" I tried to keep my cool.

"We bumped into Jake, as we left the restaurant..." My heart stopped, why, why did they have to bump into him, I thought they were in London! "Babe, you've gone quiet on me," he said, breaking my thoughts.

I swallowed, "sorry, just wasn't expecting that!"

I heard him sigh down the phone, "It bothered him seeing me with your parents. I just wished you were on my arm. His face was a picture, imagine what it would have been like if you were with me!" he laughed, "anyway beautiful, get some sleep. I can't wait to see you tomorrow."

"I can't wait to see you either, I will see you in the church, Mr Cole." I felt sick, but I didn't want him to know how I was feeling.

"Night baby, sweet dreams!"

"You too." I smiled as I put the phone down. I plugged it in to my charger cable and flopped back down on the bed. "Fuck," I muttered. Why wasn't Laura awake? This was when I needed her. I needed to talk to someone.

I contemplated texting Brooke, but I didn't want to wake her. My thoughts were going over and over in my head, I couldn't seem to shut them out. I must have laid in bed for about forty minutes before I finally fell asleep.

CHAPTER TWENTY-THREE

Like promised, Lucinda came in at seven am to wake us. I groaned, I wasn't ready to get up yet.

I felt like I had only been a sleep for a couple of hours. Laura stretched and sprung out of bed "I'M GETTING MARRIED TODAY, WOOHOO!" I couldn't help but laugh, she reminded me of Monica out of Friends on the morning of her wedding.

Lucinda returned with bacon sandwiches and a cup of tea for us both – she really was a gem. Laura came and sat next to me on the bed, "How did you sleep? Don't mean to be rude, but, you look like shit," she said bluntly while shoving her bacon sandwich in her mouth. Tyler was so lucky.

"I feel like shit," I grumbled.

She raised an eyebrow, "What's wrong? Are you not feeling well?" I could see the sheer panic on her face.

"No, no, I feel fine," I sighed, I didn't want to make her morning about me, "it's nothing really, just Carter bumped into Jake last night. Nothing was said I don't think, it's just played on my mind all night."

She dropped her sandwich in her lap, "what the..." she was just staring at me.

"I know!" I was nodding at her.

"I thought he had moved to London," she replied picking up her sandwich and shoving it in her mouth.

I just shrugged at her, "Anyway," I said, "enough about that, I'm sure the makeup artist will do wonders on my bags." I smiled, "Let's get you ready!"

She smiled at me and jumped up off the bed and ran towards her bathroom, "Don't worry about that dipshit!" she shouted as she shut the door behind her.

The bridal party was here, operation get married was in full swing. The make-up artist was working on a rota, as one was getting our make-up done, the other's hair was being styled. Laura had decided on loose, messy buns with loose curls coming down, our make-up was subtle, so it didn't look too much with our dresses.

We heard a knock on the door, and Laura's dad, Gary walked in with a big bunch of flowers "These just came for you darling," he said giving Laura a kiss on the cheek, "they are from Tyler." He welled up at the sight of his beautiful daughter, the room filled with 'ahhhs' as Laura read the card on the flowers. 'I can't wait to marry you, see you at the altar at 1pm, don't be late, love you forever and always, Tyler xx.'

Laura picked up a tissue out of the tissue box on her

dresser and gently dabbed her eyes, she then stood up and hugged her dad tight. Zoe, Brooke and I were dressed and getting the last bits together.

Lucinda was in the bathroom helping Laura get her dress on, Gary was sitting on the chair in the corner of the bedroom, all suited and booted. He looked very handsome.

Suddenly, the bathroom door opened and out walked Laura. She looked absolutely stunning - her blonde hair sat in loose curls that fell softly down past her shoulders, her piercing blue eyes glistened with happy tears, her lace wedding dress clung to her body in all the right places. A beautiful, delicate necklace sat just above the sweetheart neck, her sleeves sat just off her shoulders, the dress clung to her hips and thighs before fanning out into a slight mermaid fit, her veil was the same length as her train which slowly followed her as she made her way into the bedroom.

I wiped away some stray tears, while Gary was a sobbing into some tissue. The look on his face was priceless. Brooke and Zoe were stifling their cries and trying to keep their selves busy by making sure they had everyone's bouquets. Her mum was making sure her veil was sitting right and re-adjusted her sleeves.

I walked over to her, "Oh Laura, you are absolutely stunning!" She wiped her eyes, "You okay? You ready to go? The horse and carriage are outside."

She nodded at me.

That was my cue to get everybody rounded up and

outside.

Laura was getting married a short journey away in a manor house just outside the village, her and Gary were going in the horse drawn carriage, Lucinda, me and the bridesmaids were following up in a classic car.

We made our way downstairs and outside to the front lawn. As I had hoped, Laura sat on the swing her dad made all them years ago for a photo. Gary stood behind her beaming with pride while Laura sat there and looked pretty, the blossom falling around them, the timing was perfect. The photographer was snapping away at everything that was going on, making sure he didn't miss a moment.

Gary got into the horse and carriage first, then took Laura's hand and helped her in. I walked up and handed her the bouquet. "Let's do this!" I smiled at her, "Enjoy every moment, I love you." I blew her a kiss and waved at her as the carriage started to pull away.

As I walked back to our car, I felt someone looking at me. I held onto the door of the car and looked around, and there, standing over the other side of the road, watching my every move, was Jake. My heart stopped, I couldn't move.

"Freya, hurry up, get in the car!" Brooke moaned. "What the hell are you doing?" she shouted.

I was frozen to the spot. All of a sudden, I felt a tug on my right arm, I looked down and Brooke was staring up at me, she looked annoyed, "Get in the car, now!" she said angrily. I slowly stepped into the car and slammed the door,

"What the bloody hell was that about!?" she huffed.

I finally came back round, "Jake," I muttered.

She looked at me confused, "Jake?" she repeated.

I nodded, "Yeah, standing over the other side of the road. Watching me."

Brooke looked out the window, she must have thought I was losing it. The driver pulled away as we sat driving behind the carriage "Are you sure it was him?" she questioned, I darted her a cold glare, "Okay, okay, I was only asking!" she rolled her eyes at me.

"Look, can we just forget it? I don't want this ruining the moment. He probably just wanted to send his congratulations onto Laura and Tyler?"

Brooke didn't say anything; she just looked out the window. After a short car journey, we arrived at the venue. I gave Laura's dress and veil the once over before making our way up the stairs to the doors. Lucinda walked in before us to make sure everything was okay and to take her seat at the front, Gary was still a blubbering mess, holding onto Laura's hand tightly and not letting go.

I stood at the front, Brooke was behind me, Zoe behind her and then Laura – I wasn't quite sure why I had to stand at the front, but I didn't question it.

I took a deep breath and turned to look at Laura, "Let's do this, let's get you married!" I put on a big smile as the main doors opened.

From nowhere, the room was filled with The Piano Guys

– Perfect, all the guests stood, and there standing at the bottom with a huge grin, was Tyler. I slowly started walking down the aisle, each row end had a small arrangement of blush pink and champagne roses and there was an ivory aisle runner that stopped just before Tyler's feet. The fairy lights hanging from the beams of the manor house gave it that last finishing touch.

My eyes started scanning for Carter, I started to panic when I couldn't see him. Then there, out the corner of my eye, he was, standing next to my dad, his green eyes twinkling, his perfect white teeth showing as his smile spread across his face. He looked beautiful, his mousy brown hair messy, as usual, he was wearing a black suit, a crisp white shirt and a black bow tie, he really did look hot. He gave me a little wink as I walked past.

I relaxed as I got to the altar and stood to the left, waiting for Laura to arrive, Brooke joined me, followed by Zoe.

Gary stood next to Laura, standing proud. He kissed her hand, then kissed her on the cheek as he placed her left hand into Tyler's. He took a step back and sat next to his wife, who by this point was also a blubbering mess. As the priest asked everyone to sit, he began the ceremony. I couldn't wipe this smile off my face - I had stopped thinking about Jake, and what had happened, I was drunk on love watching my best friend get married, in a few moments they'd be married, it would be the start of her new life as Mrs Smyth.

After the speeches, people started getting up to mingle. Carter rested his hand on my thigh, "You look wonderful Freya," he said as he squeezed my leg slightly.

"As do you, I really dig you in a suit," I replied.

"Oh, do you now? Maybe I will remember that for later!" he gave me a wink. "I'm going to get a drink? Would you like one?"

I finished my wine and nodded, "Same again, please." he lent down and kissed me on the forehead, I am so glad he is here with me.

Carter returned with our drinks, I really wanted to ask him about last night, but it just wasn't the time of the place, we would speak about it tomorrow. He sat down next to me and pulled his phone out, then he opened his emails and typed a quick response. "Sorry," he said, "it's just work stuff, I need to head back tomorrow, something has come up that I need to sort before New York on Monday."

I frowned at him, I didn't want him to go, "You don't have to come with me, I can send James up on Sunday evening to get you if you would prefer," he suggested.

The wine was really starting to get to me now, "I will come with you, I don't want to stay here without you," I replied as I leant in to kiss him.

We were interrupted as the DJ spoke over the microphone introducing the new Mrs & Mrs Smyth as they walked onto the dance floor hand in hand, smiling and laughing away; Bruno Mars – Just The Way You Are started playing.

I stood up and walked over to the edge of the dance floor to watch their first dance, when I felt Carter's hands move slowly round my waist. He pulled me into him and buried his head into my neck "I really have missed you," he whispered, and I smiled.

This moment right here was perfect, the mood, the lighting, the music and Carter, of course. The DJ asked all the other couples to join the newly married couple on the dance floor. Before I had a chance to run, Carter took my hand and led me to dance. I put my arms up around his neck as his arms sat loosely around my waist, resting slightly on top of my butt.

I leant up and gave him a kiss, "Thank you for these last few days, it really has meant a lot," I said in his ear.

He leant down and replied, "You're welcome... I've really enjoyed myself," he leant in towards me, our lips meeting as we lost each other in the song. I just wanted to go home and lose myself in him.

The next morning, I woke early, my head felt fuzzy. I don't even remember drinking that much. I rolled over to see Carter laying there, snoring softly. The sun shone on his skin. I could stare at him all day. I leant across and drank my water. It wasn't until I went to the toilet and came back that I realised Carter was in my room, how the hell did he get past my dad?

I snuck back into bed and cuddled into him, I would go

downstairs in a minute - I just want to lay there for five minutes.

I woke with a jolt, I looked around to see Carter was gone, was it a dream? I looked at the clock ten am. I must have fallen back to sleep.

I jumped out of bed and ran downstairs, my heart calmed down, there he was, sitting with my mum and dad drinking tea. I didn't even know he liked tea. He was dressed, his bag sat by the door. "Morning, dear."

"Morning Mum, did you have fun last night?" I asked, she gave me the side eye.

"Yes, until you lost all control of your legs and ended up like bambi on ice," she snapped. Carter let out a laugh. "Honestly Freya, poor Carter had to bring you home!" she shook her head tutting, then gave Carter a sympathetic look. I couldn't have been that bad, she was obviously over exaggerating.

I sat down at the table and helped myself to some toast then I poured myself a strong tea. Dad smiled at me, "At least you had fun, ay baby face?"

I put my head in my hands, *why, why did I have to drink so much?* I mouthed the words 'sorry' to Carter but he told me not to worry about it, "So are you leaving already?" I asked.

He swallowed his mouthful of tea, "Well, not just yet. I'm waiting for you." Ah yes, I had decided to go back with him before New York.

"Let me just finish this tea and I will get ready," I rubbed my eyes. I had black smudged over my fingers - I obviously couldn't be bothered to take my make up off last night. I finished my tea and excused myself from the table.

I went up to my room and packed my bits away, trying to piece the events of last night. I'm normally a fun drunk, a bit scatty and clumsy, but fun. I brushed my teeth and then tackled my hair; the hair spray had made it impossible to brush. I gave up and threw it in a messy bun, put a bit of makeup on and threw the clothes on I had travelled down in. They were all washed an ironed. Like I said, Mum is a ninja when it comes to washing.

I made my way downstairs, Carter was standing at the front door waiting for me, mum and dad by his side. They seemed more upset about him going than me. I put my suitcase next to Carter's. Luckily it was only my little suitcase and not my big one that was still in the car. My mum gave me a tight hug and squeezed me, "Don't leave it so long next time darling!" she kissed me and gave me another squeeze.

"I won't mum, I'm really going to miss you both."

Dad hugged me, "We are going to miss you too sweetie," he said, getting upset. I hated seeing them upset, because I then get upset.

Mum then hugged Carter and said her goodbyes. Dad shook his hand and asked him to call him when he got home. It really seemed like those two have formed quite the bromance.

Carter opened the door and took the suitcases to the door, "Thanks for having us mum, it's been wonderful," I smiled.

Carter put my case in the boot. Just as he shut the boot down, he looked over at me, "You ready?"

I nodded.

I really hated goodbyes, especially when they were to my mum and dad. I felt bad not saying bye to Laura, but she was leaving for her honeymoon shortly, so I planned to call her once I was back home in London.

Carter walked round to his side of the car and opened the driver's door. I walked towards the passenger side when I heard a familiar voice call my name. I turned around to see Jake. He was standing outside my mum and dad's house, staring at me.

Carter got back out of the car and stood next to me. He took my hand and squeezed it. I swallowed before opening my mouth, "What do you want Jake?" I said harshly, "First outside Laura's house, and now here?" I felt Carter look at me, whoops, maybe should have told him about that.

Jake walked towards us, "I need to speak to you, please Freya, give me five minutes." I looked at my mum and dad who were just standing, staring in the doorway. He took a step closer. "Don't go!" he pleaded, I looked at him confused, "Please, don't go. I fucked up Freya, I don't want to lose you again, especially not to him!" he hissed, I felt Carter's grip tighten. What the hell was going on?

"You won't have a chance to lose me again, I've moved on, so have you. Where is she anyway? Your doting fiancé?" I snarled.

He looked at the floor and shook his head. "It's over Freya, I called it off." my mouth dropped open.

I let go of Carter's hand and took a couple of steps closer to Jake. I could see he was upset. I looked back at Carter, he had a face like thunder, "What do you mean you called it off?"

Jake let out a laugh "Has your new lover boy not told you?" he scowled.

I furrowed my brow.

"Let me fill you in, when I bumped into him last night when he was leaving the pub, Aimee changed, she said she knew him, he was an ex..." he over exaggerated the 'x.' My heart felt like it stopped, I looked back at Carter. He was staring straight through me, his eyes glazed, "Yeah, she told me they had had an arrangement, she was one of his 'flavours,'" Jake was getting really wound up, I couldn't believe what I was hearing, Aimee, the woman who Jake cheated on me with, had been with Carter, too? I could feel the tears coming, I tried to swallow 'don't cry, don't cry,' I said to myself.

I turned my back on Jake, so I was facing Carter, "Is this true?" I asked.

He didn't say anything.

"IS THIS TRUE?!" I shouted at him as loudly as I could.

Carter dropped his head in defeat, "Yes," was the only

word that came out of his mouth. It all started making sense. Carter knew that Aimee was with Jake. He was looking to get revenge. I looked at Jake, then back at Carter. "You just wanted revenge?" I snarled at him and he took a step closer to me. "Don't!" I shouted at him.

"Freya please, let me explain..."

I shook my head. I didn't want to hear it, but he kept talking anyway.

"Yes, at first, that was my plan, you were just going to be a revenge fuck, but I fell for you. I fell for you the moment I laid eyes on you in Jools's office." His shoulders dropped, he looked like a broken man. "I should have told you, but how could I explain that without sounding like a complete arsehole?"

I heard Jake snigger, the thought of both the men I have slept with and loved, standing in front of me after both being with that whore.

Carter came closer to me, I felt the shivers run through my body, "Please Freya, come home!" The tears started flowing.

Jake moved closer to me and wrapped his arms around my shoulders, I leant into him.

Carter stepped back towards the car, "Baby," he stammered, "please, I love you..." he whispered.

I looked over at my mum and dad, mum was crying, dad was holding her tight, if looks could kill both of these men would be dead right now.

I shook Jake off me and stared at Carter, he loved me? I couldn't say anything.

"I've got to go Freya, please, come with me!"

I couldn't move, I watched him slowly walk to the car and take both my suitcases out. He placed them on the path outside my parents' house. He walked back over to me and kissed me on the forehead "You know where I am, you have the flight and hotel details, please baby, I don't want to lose you."

I stood and watched him get back into the car, the engine roared as he reversed slowly just in front of me and stopped for a few seconds. I could see him looking at me in the rear-view mirror as he drove away.

There I was, standing in-between my Something New and my Something Old, completely broken and torn. My heart shattered into a thousand pieces as I watched him drive away. My head was saying the complete opposite to my heart, and for the first time, I didn't know which one to listen to.

ACKNOWLEDGEMENTS

Thank you so much for reading my book. If you enjoyed it, I would love if you could share it with your family, friends and on your social media.

I want to say thank you to my amazing husband, family and friends for being so supportive during this. Honestly, if it wasn't for them, I don't think this book would have ever got finished.

Emma, my darling. Thank you so much for helping me when I struggled, you have been such an amazing friend during this journey and the non-stop support you have given me throughout will never be forgotten. You were the first person to read it and give me your honest feedback, I will be forever grateful to you.

I would like to thank my good friend Rebecca for helping me out with the editing of this book. I honestly cannot thank you enough for your help and quick turn around.

Formatting by Leigh. Wonderful Leigh. You have been amazing, I really don't know what I would have done without you. Not only have you made my book look amazing when all it looked like was a big essay, you have made the book what it is with the wonderful cover. Not forgetting the help with how to get my book up and running, I am honestly so grateful for all of your help.